What had brought the errant Viscount Darlton home to Flaxstone, after five long years away?

Tori found herself wondering—not for the first time—as they toured the rest of the upstairs of the house, then made their way back to the wide entrance hall. Before he'd left, he'd been laid-back, funny and insatiably curious about everything to the point of serious annoyance. Since he'd returned, he was still all those things, but with a darker edge under them somehow, which she didn't quite understand. And it niggled at her, not knowing what had changed.

If she had more of an ego she'd think he'd returned purely to make her life hell, except she was certain she didn't rank that high in his thinking or priorities. Except for that one night, just before he'd left. He'd definitely been thinking about her then, as he'd kissed his way across her naked body, whispering her name against her skin in the darkness.

But that night was something she *definitely* wasn't thinking about. Ever again. It was another thing that was better left in the past.

Dear Reader,

Is there anything more festively romantic than a snowbound inn? The Moorside Inn, where Tori and Jasper get stranded for part of their story, is a composite of many wonderful English pubs, inns and boutique hotels I've had the good fortune to visit over the years. It's the sort of place that welcomes you in, sits you in front of the fire to keep warm, brings you a glass or mug of your favorite tipple, and leaves you to read your book in peace. (Not that Tori and Jasper do much quiet sitting and reading!)

I hope this story gives you the same feeling this Christmas season. The feeling of being somewhere safe, warm and welcoming, with holiday music playing softly in the background and the knowledge that, somehow, everything will be all right and love will win out. Even if it takes Tori and Jasper a while to see that...

Festive wishes,

Sophie x

Snowbound with the Heir

—

Sophie Pembroke

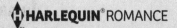

HARLEQUIN® ROMANCE

Recycling programs
for this product may
not exist in your area.

ISBN-13: 978-1-335-49965-3

Snowbound with the Heir

First North American publication 2019

Copyright © 2019 by Sophie Pembroke

All rights reserved. Except for use in any review, the reproduction or
utilization of this work in whole or in part in any form by any electronic,
mechanical or other means, now known or hereafter invented, including
xerography, photocopying and recording, or in any information storage
or retrieval system, is forbidden without the written permission of the
publisher, Harlequin Enterprises Limited, 22 Adelaide St. West, 40th Floor,
Toronto, Ontario M5H 4E3, Canada.

This is a work of fiction. Names, characters, places and incidents are
either the product of the author's imagination or are used fictitiously,
and any resemblance to actual persons, living or dead, business
establishments, events or locales is entirely coincidental.

This edition published by arrangement with Harlequin Books S.A.

For questions and comments about the quality of this book,
please contact us at CustomerService@Harlequin.com.

® and TM are trademarks of Harlequin Enterprises Limited or its
corporate affiliates. Trademarks indicated with ® are registered in the
United States Patent and Trademark Office, the Canadian Intellectual
Property Office and in other countries.

Printed in U.S.A.

www.Harlequin.com

Sophie Pembroke has been dreaming, reading and writing romance ever since she read her first Harlequin as part of her English literature degree at Lancaster University, so getting to write romantic fiction for a living really is a dream come true! Born in Abu Dhabi, Sophie grew up in Wales and now lives in a little Hertfordshire market town with her scientist husband, her incredibly imaginative and creative daughter, and her adventurous, adorable little boy. In Sophie's world, happy *is* forever after, everything stops for tea and there's always time for one more page...

Books by Sophie Pembroke

Harlequin Romance

The Cattaneos' Christmas Miracles

CEO's Marriage Miracle

Wedding Island

Island Fling to Forever

Wedding of the Year

Slow Dance with the Best Man
Proposal for the Wedding Planner

The Unexpected Holiday Gift
Newborn Under the Christmas Tree
Road Trip with the Best Man
Carrying Her Millionaire's Baby
Pregnant on the Earl's Doorstep

Visit the Author Profile page
at Harlequin.com for more titles.

For Laurie, with every possible best wish for your adventures ahead!

Hope this Christmas is your most magical one yet.

Praise for
Sophie Pembroke

"A poignant, feel-good and irresistible romantic treat that I struggled to put down, *Slow Dance with the Best Man* is a fantastic tale about second chances, healing from old wounds and finding the courage to fall in love that will touch the hearts of romance readers everywhere."

—*Goodreads*

CHAPTER ONE

TORI EDWARDS STARED up at the crenellations and chimneys of Stonebury Hall and wondered which eighteenth-century aristocrat had decided to build a house with battlements in the middle of nowhere, on the north-westerly edge of the North York Moors National Park. Who did they think they were defending themselves from out there anyway?

She supposed the answer was probably in the plastic information file she'd been given on arrival, but her fingers were too frozen to open it and check. The agent who'd welcomed them could probably have told her too, but Tori wasn't here for the guided tour. She was here to judge exactly how Stonebury Hall could be the next link in the Earl of Flaxstone's chain of profitable estates, since apparently he'd bought it without consulting her, his deputy, anyway. The agent could only tell her what the property *had* been. She needed to explore it alone to get a feel for what it *could* be.

That said, maybe she could explore *inside* for a while, on the off chance it was ever so slightly warmer away from the biting wind. She looked up at the crenellations again. The stonework matched the heavy grey of the sky, and the whole building gave off a 'go away' vibe. She had a suspicion that inside would be just as chilly.

Still, she needed to see the rooms too. Get a feel for if this building was itching to be a hotel, or a business centre, or a restaurant and tea room with craft and independent shops around it. Maybe a place for team-building retreats. Or a farm shop and café, if the land around it proved profitable. So many options... and, for once, Tori might actually get to decide what happened to the space next. Her own project, her chance to show the earl how far she'd come in his employ, that she was ready for more—more responsibility, more challenges, more independence. More life.

'This place is smaller than it looked on the agent's website.' A clipped, plummy voice swept in on the cold draught through the windows, before its owner even appeared in the room. Wasn't it just like Jasper, Viscount Darlton, the earl's only son, to assume she'd be there waiting breathlessly to hear him talk? 'Come have a look at the kitchens.'

He disappeared back through the doorway, not even waiting to see if she followed. Typical. Jasper *always* expected women to be at his beck and call—there when he wanted them, and then gone when he didn't. Just like everything else in his privileged life, she assumed.

She *did* follow him, though. Not because of his aristocratic manner, or his dark, handsome looks, or even his air of expectation and confidence. Because it was her *job*.

And because she wanted to see the kitchens. She was definitely leaning towards some sort of culinary enterprise for this place…

'Huh.' She looked around what, in a building without battlements, would have been a nice, average, farmhouse kitchen, with space for a dining table.

'See what I mean?' Jasper ran his hand over the battered wooden table in situ. 'This is more like an oversized home than a commercial property.'

A place can be both, Tori thought, but didn't say. Just those simple words would give away more of her past than she'd be comfortable with Jasper—or anyone in her new life—knowing. It was the sort of comment that would raise questions. Ones she was far happier not answering.

She'd let Jasper get too close precisely once in her life. It wasn't a mistake she intended to repeat.

'It's cosy,' she admitted instead. 'But I can still see a lot of potential here. I'm going to go check out the other rooms.'

She'd meant alone, but Jasper followed her all the same, adding his own observations about the property. To Tori's irritation, she found they often matched her own—which meant she then went out of her way to find evidence to the contrary. Apparently, five years away from Flaxstone hadn't made the earl's heir any less irritating or persistent. Or maybe she was just oversensitive to it, given the last time they'd seen each other.

Strange to think that for one night she'd honestly thought there might be more to him than the spoilt playboy he portrayed to everyone else. Stupid of her, really.

'This would be a fantastic master bedroom,' Jasper said, once they'd reached the upstairs. He crossed the room to the window—rising from Jasper's waist level almost to the high ceiling, and wide enough to fit a cosy loveseat beneath. 'Look at those views over the moors.'

Tori didn't want to look. Out of that window was just another memory she was working on forgetting. She knew what those moors looked like. She'd grown up there. And she was far happier now she was away from them, she reminded herself, in case nostalgia slipped in again just at the sight of the landscape. Living in the tiny cottage on the earl's estate, just south of York, was far more pleasant. And more than that, a sign of how far she'd come. How right she'd been to leave.

Whatever the consequences had been.

It was important to always remember that. Especially at this time of year, when the temptation to go back was so strong.

'Those clouds look heavy,' Jasper added, squinting up at the grey skies. 'Did they forecast more snow? I know they're even talking about a white Christmas.'

'That'll be good for the Christmas fair at the estate,' Tori replied. That was what this season meant to her now. Revenue and marketing potential. It was better that way.

'I was rather thinking it would be good for snowball fights.' Jasper turned away from the window with a wicked grin.

Tori rolled her eyes. 'Your father is hoping for a spectacular event this year.'

Jasper's grin fell away at her mention of the earl. Interesting.

What had brought the errant Viscount Darlton home to Flaxstone, after five long years away? Tori found herself wondering—not for the first time—as they toured the rest of the upstairs of the house, then made their way back to the wide entrance hall. Before he'd left, Jasper had been the quintessential aristocratic playboy. Laid-back, permanently amused by life, and confidently parading a selection of beautiful women through Flaxstone Hall— and never the same one twice.

He'd also been an incurable flirt, and seen Tori as a challenge, she figured, since she couldn't imagine why he'd waste time flirting with her otherwise. Not when he had all those moneyed honeys to seduce.

Since he'd returned to Flaxstone, Jasper was still all those things, but with a darker edge to them somehow, one she didn't quite understand. And it niggled at her, not knowing what had changed.

Not knowing why he'd left in the first place.

If she had more of an ego she'd think he'd left and then returned purely to make her life hell, except she was certain she didn't rank that high in his thinking or priorities. Except for that one night, just before he'd left. He'd been thinking about her then, as he'd kissed his way across her naked body, whispering her name against her skin in the darkness.

But that night was something she *definitely*

wasn't thinking about. Ever again. It was another thing that was better left in the past. She'd known better then, and she *absolutely* knew better now.

'I think we've seen all we need to see,' Jasper told the agent, who was loitering in the chilly hallway waiting for them, his hands jammed into his armpits to try and keep warm. 'Right, Tori?'

She tried to think of a reason to disagree, just on principle, but nothing sprang to mind, and it *was* cold, so she gave a short nod of agreement.

'We'll be back in touch to organise our next moves once we've shared our findings and ideas with the earl,' she said, shaking hands with the agent before they left. With the sale in the bag already, he didn't seem particularly bothered by how long that might take, or what they had planned for the place.

'My turn to drive.' Jasper held out his hand for the keys to the four-by-four as they strode across the gravel driveway to where she'd parked, an hour or more earlier.

Tori's fingers flexed around the keys in her pocket, reluctant to give them up. 'I can drive back.'

'I know you can. You drove here, after all. Which is why it's my turn,' Jasper said, with exaggerated patience.

Tori hesitated, and he sighed.

'What? Are you afraid I'll crash? Or steal you away to some secluded inn in some village and treat you to dinner—I am actually starving, though, so that one might happen.'

Depends on the inn.

But she couldn't tell him that either, so, reluctantly, she handed over the keys.

'Thank you.' Jasper's smile was wide, bright and genuine—the sort of smile only someone raised with advantages rather than disasters could smile.

It just made her resent him more.

'Come on,' she said as she opened the passenger-side door and climbed in. 'I want to get home.'

Home to Flaxstone, that was, where she could put the past firmly behind her again. Not anywhere along the way that might have once held the title of 'home'.

Because maybe once she was safely back in her bright, light and solitary cottage, she'd be able to stop thinking about the one night she'd spent with Jasper, and forget all about a dark, cosy inn out on the moors that she used to call home.

Jasper eased himself into the driver's seat and immediately turned up the car's heating. It was colder than ever out there—chillier even than his father's reception when he'd returned home to Flaxstone a week or so earlier. And Jasper hadn't honestly thought that was possible.

The earl, in all his aristocratic glory, had obviously decided that the rift in the family had to be *Jasper's* fault, rather than a result of his own behaviour. Jasper had had plenty of time to think about it over the past five years, and the only conclusion he'd been able to reach was that his father's life hadn't ever allowed for the possibility of not getting everything he wanted—so he just took it, and to hell with the consequences for everybody else.

Well. One thing he couldn't just take was his son's respect. That had been lost five years ago when he'd discovered the truth about his father—and nothing that had happened since showed any signs of the earl winning it back.

But he was done thinking about his father for the day. He'd done what he came here to do.

Coming back to the UK at all hadn't been his first choice; he was happy with the life he'd forged over in America, with the reputation he'd built up and the portfolio of work he'd created. But then his father had emailed and told him that, given Jasper's absence, he intended to legitimise his *other* son as his heir, too. The title was Jasper's by law, and Flaxstone went with the title, but everything else—the business, the money, the properties—that was the earl's to distribute as he pleased.

And apparently his illegitimate son by the housekeeper was what pleased him most. The son Jasper had only discovered existed by accident, five years ago, and the reason he'd left home in the first place.

His best friend, Felix.

Jasper hadn't come back for the money, or the property, or the business. He'd come back for his reputation and, most of all, for his mother.

And it was his mother that had brought him to Stonebury Hall with Tori.

Stonebury Hall would be the perfect home for his mother, if Jasper couldn't dissuade his father from making a big, public announcement, and the earl went through with his latest, ruinous plan. Jasper wasn't even sure his mother *knew* about Felix, or if his father had any intention of telling her before the rest of the country. His mother, lovely and loving as she was, had never really seemed to inhabit the same world as the rest of them, as far as Jasper could tell. She was perfect for opening church fetes, throwing Christmas parties and keeping their little corner of England the way things had been fifty years ago, when she'd watched her mother run her own home in a fashion that was out of date even then, but she'd never really caught up with the changing times—or shown any desire to.

But the changing times had caught up with them.

Right now, the earl was still sticking his fingers in his ears and humming, metaphorically at least, telling himself that an illegitimate son, brought up in the household, with his mother still working at the house, was nothing in this day and age. That no one would care that the boy Jasper had grown up with, whose birthday was just weeks before his own, was actually his half-brother.

That Jasper's father had been lying to him, and everyone else, his whole life.

People would care, that Jasper was sure of.

Jasper had cared, mightily, the day he'd found out—an accidental glimpse of some paperwork in his father's office that had turned out to be his updated last will and testament, detailing what he left to each of his *sons*.

That plural had nearly destroyed him on its own. Hearing the details from his own father, and realising that Felix already knew *exactly* who his father was—that was what had driven him away completely.

And now the earl was talking about legitimising Felix, handing responsibility for some of the estates over to him, since, as he put it, 'My other son seems to have disowned us altogether.'

The media was going to have a field day with that. And Jasper wanted to protect his mother from that, even if he couldn't protect himself.

She needed a retreat, a bolthole, somewhere to hide away from the media, the public, and her husband for a while. Or for ever. And Stonebury Hall would be perfect for that.

Now he just needed to convince the earl to let him make it happen. His father might be the one who decided on the estate's investments and built up the property portfolio, but the actual work of transforming these places into whatever it was they believed they could be—and make money as—was delegated to others.

And that work, that sort of huge development project, was exactly what Jasper had spent five years managing overseas. He could take it on, make it everything his mother needed. A home, perhaps with a small business involved to bring in income and give her something else to focus on. Perhaps a teashop. Or a stable yard, if the paddock at the back was large enough. He needed to examine the specifications again.

And then he needed to convince his father. Surely, once the sordid truth about him, about their marriage, was out in the world, the earl would understand that his wife needed an escape, a refuge. He wouldn't begrudge her that, Jasper was almost certain. At least, not when he saw the inevitable backlash and scandal it caused.

It was possible that the whole announcement was just a ploy to get him back in the country, Jasper mused as he eased the car onto another tiny back road that led to another back road, and another, until they finally reached something wide enough for two cars to pass without one of them ending up in a hedge. Maybe it was all a cunning plan to appeal to Jasper's pride, or even his greed, by threatening to give away his inheritance, responsibilities and status to Felix.

Which just showed how little his father knew him. He had plenty of money of his own these days, thanks to a lucrative career and some canny investments with his inheritance from his grandparents. And he took pride in the career and the life he'd forged for himself away from Flaxstone. As for the responsibilities, Felix was welcome to them, too. Living a life free from expectations, except the ones he placed on himself, had a lot going for it.

But he couldn't leave his mother alone here to be humiliated and, worse, hurt. That was a step too far. If his father was going public, Jasper needed to be there when his mother found out the truth, and he needed to protect her, spirit her away from everything that followed. Preferably to Stonebury Hall.

And he was still thinking about his father.

Shaking his head, Jasper forced himself to focus on the road, the snowflakes starting to fall in earnest outside. The woman sitting next to him.

Anything except what had brought him home.

Although, he had to admit, the line in his father's email about Tori had only added to his certainty that he urgently needed to return. He hadn't imagined she'd still even be working for his father after all this time. And just one sentence—a note about how Felix had been working closely with her on estate business— had sent his mind spiralling back to that one night they'd spent together.

The night he'd found his father's will.

The night before he'd confronted his father and learned the full, awful truth.

He'd left the country without speaking to her again, which was, he had to admit, a pretty shoddy move on his part. But then, she'd clearly regretted their night together because she'd got up early and crept out of her own bedroom, in her own cottage, to avoid him the morning after, so it wasn't entirely on him.

'So, shall we take the boring route home or the scenic one?' he asked, grinning with a jollity he really didn't feel.

Tori looked up from her phone, eyes wide. The silent journey so far apparently hadn't bothered her at all—no surprise there, really. Tori Edwards was the most closed-off woman he'd ever met, so unlike all the other women he spent time with. Well, almost all the time...

He allowed himself a real smile at the memory of the one night he'd managed to slip under her defences and find the real woman hiding behind them. Tori had more battlements than Stonebury Hall, Jasper decided, remembering a time before his life had fallen apart, when trying to breach those defences had been a kind of game for him and Felix. A challenge. Something that niggled at him until he couldn't help but strive to get her to react, to show something of her real personality—rather than those closed doors behind her eyes.

It hadn't escaped his notice that the one time he'd succeeded was the night he'd felt more wounded and open than ever before.

Maybe it was all the thinking he'd been

doing about his father, or maybe it was the snow and the enclosed space, but suddenly Jasper wanted to see if he could break through those battlements again—even if only for a moment.

'Given the snow, I'd suggest sticking to the main roads,' Tori said, her voice even, uninterested. At least, if a person weren't listening carefully.

Jasper was listening *very* carefully. Which was why he caught the faint tremor underneath her words. She cared, one way or another, and suddenly he wanted to find out which.

He needed a new challenge—a distraction from his disintegrating family. Persuading Tori Edwards to open up a little could be the perfect entertainment for a snowy afternoon.

He smiled, and began his campaign.

'The snow isn't that heavy,' Jasper pointed out, his lazy voice easy with lack of caring. 'And the main roads will be packed with drivers avoiding the more interesting routes. We could cut across the moors and make it home before the real weather rolls in.'

Tori glanced out of the car window. The clouds above definitely suggested that there was a lot more snow to come.

'The weather can be different on the moors.'

She bit down on her lower lip to dispel the memories. 'The snow might have already hit there.'

'Or it might miss it entirely.'

That didn't sound likely. But he was irritatingly right about how busy the main roads would be in this weather. If they *could* make it across the lesser-used moor roads it would be quicker—unless the snow was heavier, or too many other people had the same idea, or there was a rogue tractor or sheep blocking the road...

They were idling now at the crossroads, the junction where Jasper had to choose which path to follow. Any minute now another car would come up behind them and start beeping its horn—not that Jasper seemed bothered about holding other people up. She wasn't sure he'd ever realised that it was human to worry about *anyone* else's feelings.

Normal, empathetic people didn't leave the country for five years after sleeping with a person, and then never mention it again.

'Don't you ever take a risk?' he asked, that wicked grin she remembered too well on his lips.

That grin had got her into trouble before. Well, that grin and half a bottle of gin—stolen from the earl's drinks cabinet, of course—and a bad day that had lowered her defences, if she remembered correctly.

'Unnecessary risk is the height of foolishness.'

Of course she took risks. That was a normal part of doing business. But personal risk? That was another matter. She'd taken enough of those in the past to know what happened when the risk didn't pay off. Okay, she'd taken precisely one. But that had been more than enough to teach her a lesson.

Her single night with Jasper had just been an extra reminder. She'd known better than to get involved, however fleetingly, with someone for whom romance was basically a sport. But she'd put her fears aside and let herself believe that there might be more to him, that he might think more of *her*, only for him to prove quite comprehensively that she was as unimportant to him as she'd always imagined.

She didn't need reminding again.

'This risk is necessary,' Jasper announced. 'I'm starving, and I want to get home for dinner.'

'Your stomach is not an emergency.'

'Maybe not to you.' Jasper pulled on the handbrake and leant closer, looking into her eyes. 'Are you worried about the snow? Because if it's bad we'll turn back. Or find that secluded inn I mentioned and have some dinner while we wait it out...'

Tori tore her gaze away from his. She wasn't even going to imagine what *he* was imagining could happen between them if they did that. Jasper's determined campaign of flirtation had always been distracting, however much she knew better than to let herself fall for it. '*Not* happening. Fine. Just get us home in one piece, okay?'

'Your wish is my command, milady.' Humming a few lines from a Christmas carol, Jasper took off again—heading, of course, for the road that traversed the Yorkshire moors.

Tori hunkered down in her seat. It wasn't the snow she was scared of—not that she planned to let Jasper know that.

She knew those moors. They were her home, her playground, her life, growing up. But she'd avoided so much as driving through them for nearly eight years now. She'd made her whole life away from them—not too far away, but far enough. This was the first time the earl had sent her to look at property practically on them.

And she knew the road that Jasper would take. Knew the tiny villages and hamlets it would wend and wind through, the landmarks and features it would pass. The inn that would be sitting not far from the side of the road that they would speed past without comment, without recognising the part it had played in Tori's life. The valley they'd pass through, without any sign of the car that had crashed into the rocks there, and torn her future apart.

The car crash that had killed Tyler, the man who was supposed to be the love of her life. Even if she'd been every bit as responsible for his death as those rocks he'd crashed into.

All of that was part of the life she'd put firmly behind her for ever.

Tori tugged her coat tighter around her, feeling a chill that the fancy four-by-four's heating system couldn't hope to warm. She couldn't wait for this cursed trip to be over.

CHAPTER TWO

OKAY, THIS WASN'T working at all.

Keeping his main focus firmly on the road ahead, and the swirling snowflakes that grew heavier with every moment, meant that Jasper could only spare the briefest of glances at his travelling companion. But even that was enough to realise that any hopes he'd had of Tori opening up or even relaxing a little as they took the secluded, picturesque road through the moors were doomed. Curled up in her seat, her coat wrapped tightly around her slim body, she looked almost like a child having a sulk.

Maybe that *was* what she was doing. And Jasper had teased Felix out of enough sulks in their childhood to know how to fix that.

Except he wasn't thinking about Felix. Ever. *Think about Tori. And not crashing the car.*

Tori Edwards was an enigma. She'd appeared in his life one day and hadn't left, and despite their night together he wasn't sure he knew her any better now than the day she'd arrived.

After his father's revelation about Felix's parentage, Jasper had worried briefly that Tori was another of the earl's illegitimate children, but that fear had been quickly dispelled. And given her colouring—her pale skin, her dark hair, and her bright green eyes—he should have known better anyway. He got his own dark hair from his mother, and his eyes were his father's distinctive golden brown—the same, he realised too late, as Felix's.

Jasper and Felix had both been about to start their third year of university down in Oxford when Tori had shown up that first summer, a year into her own business degree at York, and working for the earl during the holidays. He'd claimed he'd plucked her from obscurity at some roadside inn where her talents were clearly wasted. Tori had never denied the story, but Jasper suspected that his father's desire to appear a patron, a benefactor, to a penniless girl who had just needed the right chances in life had had more to do with harking back to a previous era of aristocracy than anything else.

In truth, Jasper assumed the earl had hired Tori because she was very good at her job, patronage be damned. She'd worked hard all that summer learning the ropes at the Flaxstone estate—dealing with the groups of executives there for team building down in the woods, with the paintballing range and the go-kart track; hosting birthday parties for horse-mad little girls; serving teas and coffees in the farm café and even leading walking tours of the land around Flaxstone, up to the ruins of the old hall that had been crumbling away nicely for the last three hundred years. There had been no job she wouldn't take on, and before long she'd known more about how the estate was run than staff who'd been there for decades.

The earl, for all his many faults, had at least seen the writing on the wall for Britain's landed gentry, and had found a way to diversify the assets the Flaxstone estate gave them, making the best use of their aristocratic inheritance by turning it into a business. And once Flaxstone itself had been running consistently in the black as a commercial enterprise, he'd turned his sights on the many estates in the country that *hadn't* been so prescient—and done the same for them.

And Tori, from what Jasper could gather, had been a big part of that during his absence over the last five years.

But back when she'd first arrived, she'd been

nothing more than another girl to flirt with, a challenge when she didn't flirt back, and then a puzzle for him to solve when he couldn't get her to open up at all. He and Felix had spent that whole first summer trying to bash holes in those walls she put up; teasing her, asking every question they could think of, even trying to get her drunk on long summer nights. She'd been just nineteen to their nearly twenty-one, close enough in age that it had seemed natural they'd spent time together, even if she'd lived in the staff quarters with the casual summer staff, and they had been up at the main hall.

She had been there again at Christmas that year, organising stalls for the annual Christmas market, decorating trees and staircases in the hall, and corralling carollers. Jasper had wondered briefly why she hadn't gone home for Christmas, he remembered now. Later, he'd got the feeling that she hadn't had a home to go to.

But she'd made a new one at Flaxstone. By the time she'd graduated, Tori had earned such respect from the earl that he'd given her the gatekeeper's cottage and hired her full time, before she'd even attended graduation.

And two years later, the summer he'd found out the truth about Felix, Jasper had finally broken a small hole in those defences of hers, even if only for one night. Or maybe she'd broken a hole in his.

It had been the night that he'd found his father's will, read about a potential second son he'd never heard of. His father had been out of town for meetings and Jasper had known it wasn't a conversation he could have over the phone, so he'd resigned himself to waiting until his return the next day for answers.

But patience had never been one of his virtues.

Felix, he remembered now, had been off with some girl he'd fallen for on the summer staff, and not available for drunken oblivion. But Jasper had found Tori hanging bunting on the pop-up coffee stall she'd convinced the earl to install at the start of the garden walk.

'Don't you ever stop working?' he'd asked her, leaning against the nearest tree to watch her work. She'd been methodical, focussed, and the bunting had dipped and hung at precise intervals from the tin roof of the stall.

'When it's all done, yes,' she'd replied without looking at him.

'When it's done, I need something stronger than coffee. Join me?'

She'd turned then, looked him in the eye for a long moment, and then nodded.

He hadn't expected her to say yes, not after

so many years of telling him no at every possible opportunity. But maybe she'd seen something desperate in his eyes that evening. Seen that he'd needed her. Or perhaps she'd had her own reasons—if so, she'd never told him what they were.

They'd stolen a bottle of the earl's finest gin from his healthy drinks cupboard, and drunk most of it while talking about nothing at all. But underneath the inconsequential, and in between them, every now and then there had been glimpses, moments when her armour had slipped. Seconds when he'd been able to see that she was hurting too, even if she'd never tell him why.

Then the alcohol had taken over completely, and soon they'd been giggling their way back to her cottage, pausing only to kiss against the trees that lined the path.

And then when he'd woken up the next morning she was already gone.

Did she ever think about the night they'd spent together? She'd certainly never mentioned it again. Not that she'd had much chance. She'd crept out of her own cottage before he was even awake, and avoided him for the next day. He'd confronted his father about the will the moment he'd returned, and his world had imploded. He hadn't been thinking about anything beyond the lies he'd been told his whole life when he'd decided to leave Flaxstone, and in the end he'd left in such a whirlwind he hadn't even seen Tori again. He'd barely said goodbye to his own mother, but that was partly because he couldn't bear to lie to her about Felix, but couldn't hurt her either. She couldn't have known what sort of a man she'd married, he was sure. And if she had… then she'd been lying to him too.

He couldn't face that possibility right then. So he'd run as far and as fast as he could, until the pain had started to recede.

Since he'd returned to Flaxstone, Tori had barely acknowledged his existence, until today, when she couldn't possibly avoid it.

Jasper's gaze darted to the left again to take in her profile, pensive as she stared out at the snow. Then he focussed back on the road again.

One night. Just a few hours. That was the only time he'd ever seen behind the mask. And even now, so many years later, he couldn't help but wish he could see it again. The real Tori Edwards.

Because that flash of the real woman behind the defences had been more potent than the weeks, months or even years he'd spent getting to know anyone else.

Of course, maybe that was just because he'd spent his time getting to know the wrong women—or *not properly* getting to know far too many of them. But after his teenage experiences of love, that was enough for him. He still winced at the memory of Juliet Hawkes, the object of obsession for his teenage heart that could have ruined romance for him for life.

Still might, actually, coupled with the rubbish example his father had set him.

And now he was back to thinking about his father again. Perfect.

'The snow's getting heavier,' Tori said, suddenly sitting up straighter beside him.

Jasper blinked, and let his eyes see the falling snow, rather than blocking it out to concentrate on the road.

It really was getting heavier. A lot heavier.

He'd only picked this road because it was the first thing he'd said all day that had got a real reaction out of her, and that curious, need-to-know nature of his had made him push it forward, to see where it went, in case it led him to a better understanding of Tori Edwards.

Now, looking out at the snow, he was starting to wonder if that was the best choice.

Then he saw the tail lights of the stationary

cars ahead, and the blue lights flashing beyond them, and knew that it really, really wasn't.

Tori insisted on being the one to go and find out what was happening.

This was her land, her place, even if Jasper didn't know it. Despite the swirling snow she knew *exactly* where she was. Recognised the rises, the scars in the land disappearing under that blanket of white. She knew that tree, dead and black her whole life, but now covered in the blossom of snowflakes. She recognised that uneven stone wall, bracketing the road on one side, meandering along in nothing like a straight line.

She knew where that wall led. Knew the land it marked out. If she squinted, she could almost see the building it belonged to, rising out of the snow a little way further along the road.

The Moorside Inn.

Or, home, as she'd always known it.

Tori shivered, looking pointedly away from where she knew the inn sat, and focussing instead on the treacherous and slippery path ahead of her. It was hard by now to see where the road ended and the grass verge began, and the ground seemed to shift and move under her feet as she stepped from one to the other.

Maybe she should have let Jasper investigate instead. But more than anything she'd needed to get out of that car, breathe fresh air, and step away from his curious gaze.

Did he even remember that they'd once slept together? She wasn't sure. He certainly hadn't mentioned it since his return, and there *had* been a significant amount of alcohol involved that night.

She'd never understood what had made that night so different for them both. Well, that wasn't entirely true. She knew why *she'd* felt different that night. An unfortunate clash of an anniversary she'd been trying to forget and too many reminders that wouldn't let her. When he'd looked at her with that lost look, one she'd never thought to see on his confident and assured face, for a moment he'd reminded her of Tyler.

Later though, after much alcohol, as he'd leaned in to kiss her for the first time, she hadn't been thinking about Tyler at all. Only Jasper. Something else to feel guilty about.

Anyway. Whether he remembered or not, it was better for all concerned that they pretend it never happened, so she definitely wasn't going to bring it up.

But that didn't stop her wondering.

Not right now, though. Right now she had

to figure out what the hell was going on with this road and get off the moors before Aunt Liz or Uncle Henry came out to see what was happening on the road outside the inn.

With hindsight, she really, really should have stayed in the car. And apparently she wasn't the only one who thought so.

'If you'd get back in your car, please, miss.'

A uniformed police officer approached, looking cold and very fed up. She couldn't blame him, to be honest. She felt much the same and she'd only been out in the snow for a few minutes. 'Someone will be coming along to speak to all drivers in turn.'

'What's happened?' she called out anyway, her voice fighting against the wind and snow.

'The road ahead is blocked,' the policeman responded. 'But please, wait in your car and someone will tell you what to do next.'

I know what to do next, Tori thought as she trudged back towards Jasper and the waiting car. *Get the hell out of here.*

They could turn around. Head back to the main road and take the other route. Yes, it might take for ever, but at least they'd get home tonight. And she'd be far, far away from the Moorside Inn. As long as they got moving now, this didn't have to be a disaster.

But as she reached the four-by-four, she

could already see Jasper leaning against the car, his shoulders and hair coated with snow, talking to another police officer.

'Ah, the wanderer returns!' he said as she approached, sounding far too jolly for the circumstances.

'What's happening?' Tori shoved her hands deep into her pockets and wished her smart leather gloves were fleece-lined and warm, rather than just looking good.

'Road ahead is closed. Too much snow and ice building up, and there's a risk of rock slides in the valley from the weight of the snow.'

Tori winced. She knew that valley, almost too well. The road grew narrower as it twisted between the low hills, the sharp edges of the rock rising steeply on either side. Too much fallen snow could send rocks and stones battering down.

That valley was where Tyler had died, on a warm spring night totally unlike this one.

'We'll go back, then,' she said, shaking away the memories. 'Head back to the main road. We should have taken that route in the first place.' She shot a glare at Jasper to remind him whose fault this all was.

'Probably,' the policeman agreed, glumly. 'But it's too late now. There was an accident about half a mile back, probably not long after you passed through. No serious injuries, but the road is closed that way too while it's cleared—in fact, they've closed off this whole section from the main road until it comes out the other side of the moors. Too dangerous in this weather.'

Tori swallowed down the panic rising sharply through her throat. She couldn't afford to lose it—not here, not now, and definitely not with Jasper watching.

'Then how are we supposed to get out of here?' she asked, forcing her voice to remain even.

'Good news on that front, at least,' Jasper said, grinning even as he blinked away snowflakes from his eyelashes. Those golden-brown eyes of his shone in the light from the headlights and the policeman's torch. 'Apparently there's an inn nearby that's offered to put up all the travellers caught up in this mess. See, I told you I'd take you to a nice secluded pub for dinner!'

He was so busy congratulating himself, telling the police officer how he was a man of his word, and always looked for the silver linings, that he probably didn't even notice Tori's heart sink down out of her feet and bleed into the snow. Or maybe that was just how it felt.

All she knew was that she was trapped. That

the past she'd been running from for so long had caught her at last.

And it had brought Jasper, Viscount Darlton, along as well, just for the fun of it.

'Hell,' she muttered into the night. 'I'm in actual hell.'

'I think that would be hotter, miss,' the policeman said, with a confused frown. 'Now, if you'll excuse me.' He disappeared into the night to talk to the next car in the line.

'Shall we?' Jasper asked, crooking his elbow for her to hold. 'I believe it's this way.'

Tori tucked her hands under her arms and stepped forward without him. 'I know the way.'

If she had to face her past, she'd at least do it head-on. She owed Tyler that much.

I'm coming home, Aunt Liz.

This whole day kept getting more and more interesting.

Okay, so getting stranded in the snow on the moors wasn't exactly in Jasper's original plan for the day, but it wasn't quite the disaster Tori's face suggested it was, either. They had a nice, cosy inn to shelter in and wait out the storm, and it wasn't as if either of them had been caught in a rock slide or car accident.

So why did Tori look as if she would almost rather they had?

'Looks like we'll get that dinner at a secluded inn after all,' he joked again as they trudged their way across a snow-covered field, towards the lights in the distance. Maybe she'd missed it the first time around.

Tori didn't answer.

'Maybe there'll be steak and ale pie on the menu. I love steak and ale pie.'

Still nothing.

'And I could murder a pint of something dark and hoppy. Since it looks like we won't be driving anywhere tonight.'

She flinched at that, although he had no idea why.

Jasper sighed. This was going to be a very long night if Tori refused to talk to him altogether.

Maybe it was time to bring out the big guns. Apologising.

'Look, I'm sorry I brought us along the moors road. You were right, it was too dangerous in the snow, and we should have kept to the main roads. Where we'd probably still be stuck in an epic traffic jam, arguing over which radio station to listen to, instead of heading towards what looks like a really nice inn and hopefully some steak and ale pie. But sorry, anyway.'

He could just about make out the inn through

the snow. The sloping roof, the thick stone walls, and the warm yellow lights glowing out into the darkening sky. There was even a giant Christmas tree out front, strung with old-fashioned coloured lantern lights, the sort he remembered from his childhood.

It definitely looked like the sort of place that served steak and ale pie. And now he'd apologised, Tori would stop ignoring him and they could enjoy a nice evening together.

He turned to her, smiling—until he saw the sceptical glare on her face.

'You honestly think that was a good apology, don't you?' she asked.

Jasper blinked away snowflakes, confused. 'I mean, I said I'm sorry. So…yes?'

'You said you were wrong and should have listened to me—and then told me why actually I was wrong and you'd made the right decision even now we're stuck in the snow on the middle of the moors walking towards—' She broke off suddenly, her gaze jerking away.

'A…perfectly nice-looking inn?' Jasper finished for her, more baffled than ever.

Tori sighed, hard enough that he saw her shoulders rise and fall even in her thick, woollen coat. 'The Moorside Inn serves the best steak and ale pie in Yorkshire. Possibly the world. Henry, the cook, he won't share the recipe with anyone. You're going to love it.'

'Great,' Jasper replied. But he couldn't find the enthusiasm for it that his hungry stomach had exhibited just moments earlier.

There was something about her voice. The slow, resigned monotone.

'So, you know this place?' Knew it well, he'd guess, given her words. And her reluctance to re-enter it.

Before he'd left Flaxstone, five years earlier, he'd believed he might actually be getting to know Tori Edwards at last. To see the real girl under the mask she put up for his father and everyone else.

Now, staring at her in the snow, outside a Yorkshire inn, he admitted to himself that he didn't know her at all.

He didn't know where she'd come from, or why. He didn't know what had driven her away from her home the way he'd been driven away from his.

But he had a feeling that this might be the night he finally found out.

Tori didn't answer his question, but then she didn't need to. They were almost there, now, the windows of the inn changing from blurs of light in the distance into a clear vision of the cosy, wooden-beamed rooms inside.

And as they approached the heavy, wooden front door, it flew open, revealing an older woman in a Mrs Christmas apron, her bright red curls pinned back from her face, and a wide smile on her lips.

'Welcome, weary travellers, to the Moorside Inn! I hope we can make your impromptu stop a little more comfor…' Her words faltered mid-sentence, and so did her smile. She peered out into the snow, her gaze fixed on Tori's blank expression. 'Vicky?'

Tori sighed again, but at least managed a small smile this time. 'Hello, Aunt Liz.'

Jasper looked between the two women. Yes, he was *definitely* going to find out more about Tori Edwards tonight. But the realisation only showed him just how very little he'd known about her to start with.

Maybe it was time to fix that.

CHAPTER THREE

THE MOORSIDE WAS just as she remembered it.

As Tori pulled away from the tentative, uncertain hug her aunt gave her, she took in the inn beyond. Same wooden beams. Same gleaming pumps, polished by Uncle Henry every night after he'd finished in the kitchen, ready to serve local ales to visitors. Same battered, rustic oak tables and mismatched chairs. Tyler's paintings still on the walls. Same feeling of shame, guilt and of being a disappointment as she stood there.

'We got snowed in on the road, about quarter of a mile away,' Jasper said, looking with far too much interest between her and Aunt Liz. Tori curled in on herself, as much as she could when wearing so many layers. This place was her past, another life almost. She didn't want to share it with anyone from her new life.

Especially not Jasper.

'Of course, you must be freezing! Come on in.' Aunt Liz ushered them both inside as if they were normal paying customers.

Jasper took the opportunity to raise his eyebrows at her and mouth, 'Vicky?' She ignored him. She supposed it was too much to hope for that he'd missed that use of her old, other nickname.

She was Tori now. That was all that mattered.

The things Vicky had done… She didn't want to be that person any more. The person who'd caused Tyler's death.

But family…they always remembered who you were, even once you'd become someone new. She'd always be Vicky to Aunt Liz and Uncle Henry, even if they weren't actually *blood* family. They were the closest thing she'd had for an awful lot of years now.

They walked into the bar proper, the one she'd only glimpsed through windows in the door, and suddenly Tori noticed something that *was* different about the place.

It was packed. Every table, chair, bar stool and window seat was occupied. Tori was certain she'd never seen so many people within the walls of the Moorside Inn ever before.

'I guess we weren't the only ones to get stranded, then?' Jasper said, and Aunt Liz laughed.

'Not by a long shot! That road out there is treacherous in the snow.' She shot Tori a look. 'I would have thought you would've remembered that, Vicky.'

There it was. That not so subtle reminder of why she'd left. Well, no. Why she'd never come back.

She couldn't bear to look at this place without Tyler in it. Couldn't take the pain and the grief—and most of all the pity. Pity from people who should be hating her, blaming her, and only didn't because she was too cowardly to tell them the whole truth.

Only now it seemed she had no choice but to be there.

'That was my fault,' Jasper jumped in. 'Tori—Vicky—tried to tell me to stick to the main roads, but I didn't listen. Always thinking I know best, that's my problem.'

He sounded so sincere, so disarmingly charming, that Tori could see Aunt Liz melting in front of her. Did he really believe that about himself? She doubted it. But he had at least taken the heat off her, which she appreciated. And it was worlds better than his first attempt at an apology outside in the snow.

'Well, I hope you'll know better next time,' Aunt Liz said, as if she were letting a small child off the hook for something.

'Definitely,' Jasper agreed, nodding. 'Now, I don't suppose you have any of that steak and ale pie you're famous for around here somewhere?'

Tori rolled her eyes. Thinking with his stomach. Why wasn't she surprised?

'Or perhaps we can help you get everyone here settled and sorted?' she suggested. 'I mean, unless you've changed things a lot around here I can probably still locate enough blankets and pillows for everyone.' The Moorside only had a handful of bedrooms it hired out for guests, so people were definitely going to have to share. But if they set up a dormitory sort of arrangement in the restaurant part of the inn, there should just about be enough room for everyone. They'd done it before, Tori remembered vividly, on nights like tonight when the roads were closed by weather or accidents and people got stranded. Including, once, the national rugby team during a particularly violent storm, when their bus had broken down. If *they'd* all fitted in snugly, so would tonight's guests.

'And Jasper here can help Uncle Henry in the kitchens,' Tori added. 'Since he's so concerned about the menu tonight.'

Of course, her altruistic plan also meant she could escape from close quarters with her family *and* her colleague, something she was sure they'd both noticed. Tori didn't care. She needed some space—and that, she knew, was hard to come by in the community-spirited world of the Moorside Inn.

'That would be very helpful,' Aunt Liz said carefully. 'Although you're here tonight as a guest…'

Tori shook her head. She'd never be a guest at the Moorside. It was too much a part of her. 'I want to help. And so does Jasper.' She nudged him with her elbow until he nodded.

'In that case, if you could set up the dormitory in the restaurant, like we did that time they closed the roads and we had the—'

'England rugby team staying,' Tori said along with her. 'Absolutely.'

As she turned away to go and find blankets and pillows, she could hear Jasper talking as Aunt Liz showed him to the kitchens. 'The England rugby team? Now, that I want to hear more about…'

Tori stepped through to the empty restaurant and breathed in the silence. Perfect.

This was going to be a very long night. She could feel it. And she needed a little personal space before she faced it.

Especially before she had to talk to Uncle Henry.

* * *

Tori's Aunt Liz led Jasper through the mass of people gathered in the main bar, behind the bar itself, and through a door that took them along a narrow passageway and down a short set of stairs into the kitchens. Jasper took in everything as they walked, especially the dramatic paintings that lined the walls—all slashes of dark greens and browns and purples, showcasing the landscape of the moors at its most impressive.

This place felt almost a part of the landscape itself, he realised. As if it had been here as long as the rocks and rises.

He ached to know what could have driven Tori away from it. What secrets she was hiding behind those emotional battlements.

Were they as all-consuming as his own?

And another, niggling question that had been at the back of his mind for five long years, before emerging for re-examination tonight: Did she already *know* his secrets? She and Felix had always been friendly, far more than she had been with him. *Felix* had known. Had he told her?

Jasper had to admit to himself that it seemed unlikely. But Tori was good at keeping secrets, that much was obvious. If she *did* know about

Felix, Jasper was sure she was very capable of keeping it from everyone—including him.

'Henry?' Liz called out as they entered the kitchens. 'Brought you some help.'

A large, grey-haired man, broad at the shoulder and his head almost grazing the lower of the ceiling beams, ducked out from a side room that, from what Jasper could see, appeared to be full of freezers and fridges. He was wiping his hands on a clean tea towel.

'Help? Think I'm too old and slow to do this on my own?' He smiled as he said it, though, so Jasper was almost sure it was a joke.

'Not me.' Liz jerked her red curls in Jasper's direction. 'He arrived with Vicky. *She* thought he might be able to give you a hand down here.'

Henry stilled, the tea towel taut between his hands, his white knuckles giving away his reaction to Liz's news even though his expression didn't change. 'Vicky's here?' The words were barely more than a whisper.

'We, uh, got caught up in a road closure on the moors,' Jasper explained. 'A crash behind us and a chance of the snow bringing down rocks on the valley ahead.'

'I know the place.' Henry's words were clipped. 'Police direct you here with all the others, did they?'

'That's right.'

Henry sighed. 'Too much to think she'd come back of her own accord, I suppose. So, what are you, then? Fiancé? Boyfriend?'

'Colleague,' Jasper corrected him quickly. He could just imagine Tori's face if he let her family believe there was anything more between them.

However much he might enjoy remembering the night when there *was*.

'Humph.' Henry sounded faintly disbelieving. Oh, well, that was Tori's problem. He'd told the truth. She hadn't told him *anything*.

'So, what can I do around here? Tori's setting up beds somewhere, I guess.'

'Tori, is it?' Henry asked. 'Well. You can help me pack up these ploughman's boxes for our unexpected guests. Each one gets one of each of the things set out on the table. Should be simple enough.' The words 'even for you' were unspoken, but Jasper couldn't help but hear them anyway. He got the feeling that, arriving in Tori's company, there was nothing he could have done to make a good impression on her uncle.

But that wasn't going to stop him trying, all the same. After all, how else was he going to uncover some of those secrets Tori was still hiding? If there was even a chance she knew his—and even if she didn't yet, she would soon if his father got his way—he wanted to know some of hers too. That was only fair, right?

'I'm sure I can,' he said with a grin, and picked up the first of the plastic boxes and started work.

Each ploughman's box got a hunk of bread, some cheese, a thick slice of ham, a small pot of chutney, an apple and some celery.

'I've got a giant pot of soup heating too,' Henry explained. 'We can take that up and dish it out in cups, to help people warm through. It's not much, but—'

'It's more than any of us would have got stuck out on the roads in this snow,' Jasper interrupted. 'And I'm sure they'll all be as grateful as I am for it.' Even if he still lusted after the steak and ale pie Tori had promised was the best in the county. Maybe he could come back another time and try it. In better weather.

'Humph,' Henry said again, but this time he sounded more mollified. 'So. If you're Vicky's "colleague" what sort of work have the two of you been up to?'

He was in tricky waters here, Jasper realised suddenly. If Tori hadn't been home for who knew who long—maybe since she first showed up at Flaxstone—then her aunt and uncle probably didn't know she was working for the earl.

Or that she had stayed so close to home. How much would she forgive him for giving away?

'We were visiting a property that our…boss is looking to invest in, up at the north of the moors.' That was neutral enough, wasn't it? 'Tori didn't mention that she had family so close though, or I'd have suggested we stop by without the snow forcing us on you.'

Henry barked a laugh at that. 'Which is exactly why she wouldn't tell you, I'd wager.'

'She does like to keep her cards very close to her chest.' Jasper watched Henry carefully, looking for the right way in, to get the man to tell him something, *anything*, that would explain the strange feeling that had settled over the place since they'd arrived.

There was so much to this story that he didn't know. And Jasper *hated* not being in full possession of all the facts, always had. Especially since everything had gone down with Juliet, and he'd discovered that everyone else in his world had known a lot of truths about her that he, as her boyfriend, also should have known—but hadn't. How could he possibly make good decisions if he didn't know what he was basing them on? Telling Juliet he loved her, for instance, had been a spectacularly bad one.

Especially since it had turned out *she* had

been in love with his friend Fred, and everyone else had known it. At nineteen, it had seemed the worst thing that could possibly happen to a guy.

But right now, he wasn't thinking about the past. He was trying to decide how far he could push Tori to tell him her story. To let him in.

Maybe it was just the residual instinct to push at those walls of hers, that instinct that had plagued him since they were both barely more than teenagers. Or maybe it was something more—the sadness in her eyes that he'd only really noticed since his return. Or the way she bristled whenever he said anything at all…

Whatever it was, he needed to solve the puzzle of Tori Edwards. And here was her uncle, holding the key.

But all Henry said was, 'She has her reasons. Heaven knows the girl has never talked when she doesn't want to. She'd always run away instead, even as a child. Hide in the strangest of places, until…well, until someone found her. Now, are you done with those boxes?'

Jasper nodded, his mind occupied with Henry's words. And the certainty that he'd been about to say a name there, when he was talking about who usually found her. What had stopped him?

Or rather, who?

'Let's carry these up, then.' Henry hoisted the first, heavy tray of ploughman's lunch into his arms, and Jasper followed suit with the second. 'We'll come back for the soup.'

'If my arms can take it,' Jasper muttered, staggering a little on the stairs. But he knew he'd do whatever Henry told him to, really.

He'd do whatever it took to unravel the mystery of Tori Edwards.

The advantage of being on home turf was that Tori knew all the best hiding places. Add in the associated chaos of having far too many people crammed into the building, all needing something all the time, and keeping busy enough to avoid any difficult discussions with Aunt Liz and Uncle Henry, or questions she didn't want to answer from Jasper, was almost too easy.

Henry had sought her out as she'd laid down bedding in the restaurant. He'd watched her from the doorway for a moment or two, she suspected, before she'd turned around and spotted him. Then, he'd thrown his arms around her and held her tight, whispering into her hair that it was good to have her home.

He'd smelled of spicy vegetable soup and the Moorside kitchens, and the scent was so familiar she could almost believe that she'd never gone away at all. Then he'd stepped away and headed back to the bar without another word, and suddenly she felt every inch of the gulf between her and her family all over again.

A gulf created by her own secrets, and their shared loss.

It had been eight years. Eight years since Tyler died, eight years since she left. Was it time to tell them the truth about why? Tori knew in her heart she wouldn't. Too many painful memories for them all. The best outcome she could hope for if she *did* tell them about the last few months of Tyler's life was that she'd end up tarnishing their memories of him, as well as giving them more reasons to be angry with her. Nobody won anything that way.

Better to keep all those secrets inside, where they couldn't hurt anyone but her.

At least, with so many people crowded in eating their soup and ploughman's, there was no need for a sit-down family meal and all the awkwardness that would follow—as much as Tori would have loved one of Henry's home-cooked meals. She smiled at the sight of Jasper handing out soup from behind the bar, for all the world like one of the college students Liz and Henry used to hire to help out over the summer, before Tyler and then Tori were old enough to take their place.

There were about nine groups of people staying at the Moorside, she counted, watching over the bar. Mostly families of three or four, although there was one multigenerational set of seven, too. A couple of couples, and two sole business people—and Jasper and Tori.

She hoped they had enough beds.

As one of the children in the family nearest to her started yawning, then nodding off into her apple slices, Tori crouched down next to them and asked if they'd like to be taken through to get settled in one of the bedrooms. The largest guest room at the front of the inn would just about fit them all, she decided, and it made sense for those with younger kids to have the actual bedrooms.

The parents smiled gratefully and, clearing their dishes to the bar, followed her up the rickety stairs to the guest rooms.

Tori made a point of not looking down the narrow corridor that led to the family rooms as they passed. For all she knew, Liz and Henry might have converted her tiny single room—and Tyler's slightly larger room, for that matter—into more guest accommodation, or even an office for Liz to do paperwork in. She'd never know, because she wasn't going to ask and she definitely wasn't going to go and look.

Too many memories down that corridor.

By the time she made it back downstairs, Liz had already shown most of the other guests to rooms upstairs, or to the makeshift dormitory in the restaurant. Jasper was wiping down the bar, and Henry was pouring himself a pint.

Tori's heart contracted at the familiar sight of her aunt and uncle going about their evening, as if nothing had changed in the last eight years. Or even the last day, as the inn had been invaded by stranded travellers. Even Jasper seemed strangely at home in a place she could never even have imagined seeing him before today.

'Well, I'd better go grab a bedroll in the restaurant before they're all gone,' Tori said, as cheerfully as she could. It was late, they were all tired. Surely no one would call her out on wanting to avoid Awkward Question and Family time right now, would they?

But Liz, glancing up from wiping down tables, gave her an odd look. 'I've kept your old room free for you and Jasper,' she said. 'I know it's not big, but it'll be more private than sleeping with the hordes in the restaurant.'

'Quieter too,' Henry added. 'Some of those kids had a real set of lungs on them.'

Tori had heard. She'd hoped that if she couldn't sleep, as she often couldn't, the sound of the kids' shrieks would at least distract her from her own thoughts.

But now it seemed all she'd have to distract her was Jasper. And she knew from past experience that he could be far too distracting by half.

'Jasper and I are just work colleagues, Aunt Liz,' she said, in case her family had got the wrong idea. Whatever else they'd shared once, briefly, it was long gone. And whatever she thought she'd seen in him that night, she knew now she'd only imagined it. She was pretty certain he'd have spent the last five years flirting with any woman who caught his eye, seducing plenty of them and then moving on. Just as he'd done with her, and plenty of others before her.

Her love life was depressing enough without adding 'fell for Jasper's seduction line and got abandoned *twice*' to her romantic résumé.

'That's what I told them,' Jasper said, with a shrug. 'But to be honest, at this point, a bed is a bed and I'm knackered.' He tossed his towel over the rail on the bar, raised the section of wood to let himself out, then crossed towards her. 'So, lead on, roomie.' He flashed her an obnoxious grin that was both annoying and weirdly reassuring. Everything else felt wrong and out of step tonight, but at least Jasper was still Jasper.

Tori wasn't sure she should find that as comforting as she did.

She just hoped that when Liz and Henry had renovated the room they'd added bunk beds, or something. Otherwise they were in for a very awkward night indeed.

CHAPTER FOUR

'I COULD SLEEP on the floor,' Jasper said, eyeing the bed with annoyance. Was it even a full single? It didn't look it. To be honest, it didn't look all that much more comfortable than the wooden floor beside it, but he supposed at least with shared body heat it might be warmer. The ancient stone walls of the Moorside Inn didn't seem to do much in the way of retaining heat, this far from the fire roaring in the grate downstairs in the bar. Even this tiny bedroom—not much wider than the bed itself, and with space for just a small bookcase and chair at the end, by the door—was icy cold.

'If you freeze to death on my watch your father will fire me,' Tori said, ever practical.

'Nice to know my well-being is of such great personal concern to you,' Jasper replied. At least she was still being snarky. He'd be really worried about her, otherwise.

Oh, who was he kidding? He was worried about her anyway.

Back home at Flaxstone Tori was always aloof but in control. Here, at the Moorside Inn, she seemed…jumpy. As if she was dashing from one thing to the next so she didn't have to stop and look around, take anything in.

Or talk to her family.

Yeah, he could totally get that part of it. It was pretty much exactly what he'd been doing since he came home, too. His father didn't deserve his time or attention. And as for his mother…he just didn't know what to say to her. How much she already knew, or, if she *did* know, how she felt about the discovery that her husband's illegitimate son had been living under her roof since he was born. He needed to have a proper conversation with her, soon, but his mum had always lived stubbornly in her own world, one that was extinct outside her mind, and Jasper knew he had to time it properly.

Which only really left him Tori to talk to at all. Well, Tori and Felix, but one of those two had lied to him for the last decade and a bit, so he was fine with ignoring him too.

But he couldn't exactly ignore Tori. Not when they were sharing a bed the size of a postage stamp for the night.

'I mean it,' he said, not meaning it at all. 'I can take the floor.'

Tori looked over her shoulder at him, half-way through stripping off her suit jacket. 'Look,' she said, with a weary sigh. 'Nothing that has happened since we left Stonebury has been exactly…optimal, but it's where we are. Let's just get through it, get out of here tomorrow, and pretend this whole day never happened, okay? Even the part where we have to share my childhood bed to make sure neither of us catches pneumonia.'

Okay, now he was really worried about her. She wasn't even protesting at the idea of having to share the bed with him. This was not the Tori he knew.

The Tori he knew would have stolen his coat as an extra pillow then shoved him onto the floor.

This was actually getting a bit unnerving now.

Cautiously, Jasper stripped off his jumper, shirt and jeans, leaving his T-shirt and boxers on for Tori's sake. And warmth. In fact, he was reconsidering the jumper; it was absolutely freezing in this room.

'How did you make it through childhood without freezing to death in here?' he asked, turning back to find Tori already tucked up under the covers, holding them close to her chin.

She shrugged, the brightly patterned duvet moving with her shoulders. 'Mum and I didn't move in until I was eight. I guess I was past the delicate stage by then.'

Jasper wasn't sure if she realised it, but that was the most she'd ever told him about her life before Flaxstone.

Rather than draw attention to what she'd said, he slipped under the duvet beside her, tugging it to get her to release enough to actually cover all of him. The bed was an excruciatingly tight fit, and the duvet far too small for two grown adults anyway. Jasper shifted self-consciously to try and get comfortable while still maintaining an acceptable distance between them, forcing himself not to think about the last time he'd been this close to Tori Edwards.

He'd been younger then. Stupider. Lost and unsettled and in need of something real, something grounding. Like Tori.

And she'd been…beautiful. Soft to touch and melting in his arms, under his kisses and— He really needed to *not* be thinking about this. If she got the slightest hint that he was—and his body was more than ready to give that to her if he let it—then he'd be on the floor faster than an avalanche, even if his father *did* fire her for letting him freeze to death.

Which he was pretty sure he wouldn't. He got the impression that, these days, Tori and Felix were more his father's children than he was. Not that he cared.

'Oh, for heaven's sake.' Suddenly, Tori twisted under the duvet, reaching around to grab his hand and pull him close against her back, curved around her body like a question mark.

Jasper took a lot of deep, calming breaths.

'Trust me, there is no other way for two people to get any sleep in this bed together,' she said, her words muffled against the single pillow.

'Speaking from experience?' He wasn't sure he liked the idea of Tori in this bed with another guy, even if she wasn't really there *with* him now.

'I wasn't always eight,' she said, caustically. 'I was eighteen when I left this place.'

Why? The question battered at the inside of Jasper's skull, desperate to get out. But he knew Tori better than that—even if he was realising by the moment that he didn't know her as well as he'd thought. She'd never tell him, and it would only make the whole situation more awkward.

But maybe she'd tell him something else.

'What made you move in here with your aunt and uncle in the first place?' Maybe she'd be more comfortable talking about those long-ago, and hopefully happier, times.

'They're not really my aunt and uncle,' Tori said, her voice blurry with encroaching sleep. 'Liz was my mum's best friend since primary school. When my dad left us… Mum brought us here and Liz and Henry took us in without questions. Mum worked the bar, or the kitchens, whatever they needed. And she baked cakes and things for the local mums' groups in the village who started meeting here for coffees on weekday mornings. She ran a book club, a babysitting circle…she really made this place home.'

It sounded idyllic. But something in Tori's exhausted voice told him the ending wouldn't be quite so happy.

'When she died, Liz and Henry kept me anyway. It was that or foster care, and Liz wouldn't let that happen.'

'How old were you?' His heart hurt at the pain in her voice. He knew she wouldn't be telling him any of this if it weren't for the situation and the lateness—it was always easier to talk in the dark, and this snow-buffeted, muffled night was darker than most.

But he couldn't help but be grateful for this glimpse behind the barricade.

'Fourteen,' Tori said. 'It was a long time ago now. Nearly half my life.'

But Jasper would bet money she still thought about it every day. That it still caused her pain, all the time.

'When was the last time you were here?'

'Eight years ago. Before I came to Flaxstone.' Her voice was slurring, sleep overtaking her. He was almost certain she wouldn't have given him such an easy, honest answer otherwise. She was speaking on autopilot now.

He was about to ask something else, to really push his luck and the power of the moment, but then Tori's breathing changed, and when he peered over in the thin light coming under the door from the corridor outside, he could see her eyes were closed, her mouth a little open as she slept.

The moment was gone. And it was probably just as well. He didn't want her regretting tonight in the morning—the way she obviously regretted the last night they'd spent together, albeit for different reasons. Even if, at the time, she'd been a more than enthusiastic participant.

He slumped back against the mattress, keeping his careful position around Tori's body, and closed his eyes. He should sleep too. It had been a long day, and who knew how tomorrow would pan out?

But he couldn't stop wondering what could have been so awful it had driven Tori away from the home and the people who had taken her in and loved her when she had no one else.

Tori awoke with her nose and cheeks freezing and the rest of her...pleasantly warm. Cosy, even. Cocooned in blankets and—wait.

Her muscles tensing, she slowly turned her head to look behind her. She'd just pat around with her hands but, if her memory was right, she didn't want to risk finding out what parts of a person her fingers might accidentally come into contact with...

Jasper's aristocratic profile was irritatingly perfect in the blurry, morning light. The sun must still be on its way up over the horizon outside, but the whiteness of the world after the snowstorm made the early light brighter than it would otherwise have been. The whole world felt muted, muffled, as if they were protected away in a cotton-wool landscape where nothing could ever hurt them.

Except she was in her room at the Moorside, in bed with Jasper, so clearly that couldn't possibly be true.

He breathed in, deep and sudden, and Tori realised she was staring. But really, who could blame her? She'd never get away with studying him like this while he was awake. He'd tease her for all eternity about it—or read more into it than there was. He was an attractive man. Those long, dark lashes against his cheek. The fall of his black hair against his forehead. His neck, sloping to meet strong shoulders somewhere under the blanket…not to mention everything else that was covered out of sight, but that she could still feel pressed up against her sleep-heavy body. She was, you know, human. She noticed these things.

Which didn't mean she was going to do anything about it. This time.

Besides, while she was studying him, she wasn't remembering all the secrets she'd given up to this man in the anonymous dark the night before. Wasn't worrying about how he might use those secrets, either.

At least she hadn't told him everything. So, he knew about her mother. Knew about her father, too.

He didn't know about Tyler. That was the important thing.

The only people in the world who knew about Tyler were Aunt Liz, Uncle Henry and herself—and even they didn't know all of it.

The most awful, terrible parts. And Tori knew she needed to keep it that way.

She couldn't bear the guilt, otherwise.

Beside her, Jasper stirred, and she quickly snapped back into position facing away from him, before he caught her staring. Now she wasn't focussing on his face, she could hear the inn coming to life below them. She supposed that no one would have slept particularly well, however exhausted they were after a difficult day. Everyone was waiting to move on—for the roads to open, the snow to clear. To return to their real lives.

Just like her. Because none of this—not this place, not her family, and definitely not sharing a bed with Jasper—felt at all like the Tori she'd become since she walked away from the Moorside and never looked back.

Conscious of Jasper starting to move behind her, Tori slipped out from under the duvet and winced as her bare feet hit the cold floor. Still, frostbite was still less alarming than actually waking up in bed with him again.

Last time that had happened, she'd run before he'd woken up at all. And they'd been in her bed. Finding herself outside, barely dressed and without her phone, purse or keys had been awkward—as had climbing back in through her bathroom window later that day—

but still less awkward than sharing a morning after with Viscount Darlton.

Tori wasn't sure what it was exactly about Jasper that rubbed her up the wrong way—*or the right way*, her mind added unhelpfully—but she thought it might have something to do with his eyebrows. The way they twitched up in a quizzical manner whenever she spoke, as if he was trying to find the truth behind her words. As if he was trying to *understand* her.

Only one person had ever really understood Tori, and he hadn't liked what he'd discovered, in the end. She had zero reason to think Jasper would be any different from Tyler, in that regard. And given how badly it had gone last time…being understood was not a phenomenon she wished to repeat in a hurry. Or ever.

Liz and Henry already saw too deep, too much. They knew her, and maybe even what she was capable of. She had no idea how much Tyler had told them, while she was gone. Maybe they already knew everything, after all. Another reason she wasn't exactly keen to extend the family reunion. She liked her secrets hidden at best, or at least unspoken.

Time to go.

Wriggling back into her clothes at speed—it was too damn cold out to risk another half-dressed escape—Tori kept one eye on Jasper as he stirred again, one arm flung over his eyes as he flipped to his back and started to stretch. Definitely waking up.

Grabbing her boots to put on later, Tori slipped out of the bedroom door, checking the corridor was clear before padding down the stairs. Hopefully, Liz and Henry would be busy enough with their unexpected guests that they wouldn't notice her sneaking out.

She was in luck. Dodging a couple of small children racing out of the restaurant dormitory, she manoeuvred herself towards the exit and, pulling on her boots, back into the snow. The knee-high leather boots weren't really suitable for the snow, but neither was the suit she'd worn to tour Stonebury the day before. But they were the only clothes she had with her, so they'd have to do.

The guilt landed on her within the first few snow-crunching steps, but guilt was a feeling so tied into her connection with the Moorside Inn she found it easy enough to shrug off. Yes, she should have stayed to help Liz and Henry serve breakfast to the other stranded travellers, but she had at least left them Jasper as a dogs-body. And besides, she just couldn't stay there a moment longer, fighting off the memories.

She'd just walk as far as the road, she decided, and find out what the situation was.

If she was really lucky they'd already have opened it—although she suspected someone would have been up to the inn to tell them that already if they had. But perhaps they'd be close to doing so. Perhaps she'd be able to return to the Moorside with the good news that they'd all soon be free to get on their way again.

But she should have known better than to hope for that sort of luck.

'Can't see them opening it today, to be honest,' the young policeman guarding the police cordon told her. 'There's more snow scheduled this afternoon for a start, and there's already been a mini rock slide in the canyon.'

'What about opening it the other way?' she asked, a little desperate. If they couldn't cross the moors the quick way, surely they could go back the way they'd come and escape to the main roads?

But the policeman shook his head. 'Too much snow. They've closed it that way too, right back at the turn off from the main road, to stop anyone else stupid enough to try and cross the moors in this weather.' He seemed to realise what he'd said a moment too late, as his cheeks turned even pinker than they already were from the cold, but Tori waved away his stuttered apology.

She didn't care what some stranger thought about her plan—or, actually, Jasper's plan—to take this road. The only people alive whose good opinion mattered to her were her business associates, and her aunt and uncle.

And *they* probably weren't thinking lovely thoughts about her for skipping out this morning.

With a sigh, Tori turned away from the road and trudged back to the inn, pulling her phone from her pocket and dialling as she walked.

'Tori? Everything okay?' Felix's voice came sharp over the line as he picked up on the first ring. 'I got your text last night, but it didn't make a lot of sense…'

Probably because she'd said as little in it as possible. Felix was a friend, a good one. But he didn't know about the Moorside or her family, and she had no intention of telling him now.

'Everything's fine,' she said, calmly. 'Like I said in my text, we got caught in the snow and a road closure, so stayed the night at a local inn.' She took a deep breath. 'And it looks like we might be stuck here a little longer, too. Apparently it could be tomorrow before the roads are clear again.'

'So you and Jasper are stuck in the middle of nowhere together?' Felix barked a laugh. 'Well, try not to kill each other, yeah?'

'No promises,' Tori said dryly. 'Can you let the earl know what's happening?'

'Yeah, of course. Now, while I have you, I had a couple of questions about the set-up for the Christmas market...'

By the time she hung up, the inn was almost in sight again. At least the fresh air had cleared her head a little—and she'd escaped from an awkward morning-after-the-revelations-before moment with Jasper.

She wondered how he was coping with being cooped up at the Moorside with all those families and kids. He'd grown up in Flaxstone Hall, probably with a whole suite of rooms to call his own, and the ballroom to use as a playroom. The Moorside, with its low ceilings and poky rooms—and especially in its current state of overcrowding—wasn't at all what he was used to. Last night it had all still been a game to him. Tori suspected that by this morning he'd be losing patience.

But as the inn came fully into view, so did Jasper, his head visible above the wall that surrounded the grounds of the Moorside. His companions, however, were hidden by the snow-covered stone.

She could hear them, though.

'Jasper! Jasper! Use my scarf for the Mummy

snowman!' one of the kids chattering around him called.

'But then your neck will get cold,' Jasper pointed out, taking off his own scarf and wrapping it around the neck of his snow creation.

There was a whole row of them, Tori realised, of varying shapes and sizes. Big snowmen, little snowmen, and something that might have been a snow dog, with a stick in its mouth.

'How long was I gone?' she asked as she reached Jasper's gang, still amazed at the sight of Viscount Darlton playing with a horde of little kids. 'We seem to have been invaded in my absence.'

Jasper looked up at her voice and gave her a careful smile. It hadn't escaped his notice that she'd done a runner this morning again, then.

'The grown-ups are all eating breakfast inside,' he explained. 'But kids eat fast, and it just seemed cruel to keep them all cooped up when there was all this snow out here to play with.'

Tori raised her eyebrows. 'If all the grown-ups are inside, what does that make you?'

He shrugged, and this time his grin felt real. 'Maybe I'm just young at heart.'

Handing a carrot that she imagined he'd filched from the kitchen to the tallest of the children, Jasper moved past the crush to join her by the wall, calming their groans of complaint with a promise that he'd be back to play more soon. 'You went to check the road?'

Tori nodded. 'Still closed. Both ways. The policeman I spoke to reckons it won't be open until at least tomorrow; there's more snow forecast for this afternoon, but hopefully temperatures might rise after that.'

Jasper looked back over at the kids playing by the snowmen. 'Looks like I'd better come up with some more activities to keep this lot entertained, then.'

Pushing away from the wall, he headed back to his little gang, clapping his hands together and asking, 'Who reckons they can take me in a snowball fight?'

As a dozen hands went up, and Jasper used the distraction to toss the first soft snowball at the nearest kid, Tori laughed, despite herself.

This was *definitely* a side of Jasper she hadn't expected to see this week.

Then she turned to go inside and saw Uncle Henry waiting for her, and her smile disappeared again.

Time to face the music.

CHAPTER FIVE

JASPER'S FINGERS WERE taped together for the thirteenth time. The little girl—Sasha—sitting on his right stifled a giggle as she looped another strip of paper perfectly through the last circle, selected a piece of tape from the edge of the table beside them and taped it in place, another brightly coloured loop in the paper chain.

'Obviously this is a job for little fingers,' Jasper said as he shook off the tape again. But he reached for the next paper strip anyway, and fed it dutifully through the loop and taped it in place.

All around him, Christmas music hummed softly from the speakers hidden behind the ceiling's wooden beams, the sound of jingle bells and children's choirs ringing. A fire crackled and popped cheerily behind a fireguard—and far away from kids with kindling—and an old, skinny greyhound lounged in front of it, clearly happy with its lot. Outside, snow was falling again; big, fat flakes that tumbled onto the already white-covered ground. The sun had already started to dip behind the horizon, and Jasper knew that soon Henry would want to start on dinner, and that he would go and help again, because at least that way he was being useful, he was doing *something* in this world of forced inactivity.

Across the room, Tori's Aunt Liz sat cutting festive wrapping paper into strips to add to their piles, smiling at him approvingly. All around him, industrious kids were adding to the, to quote Sasha, 'most epic paper chain in the history of paper chains'. Jasper suspected it would loop around the whole pub several times over by the time they were done.

The kids' parents sat at the bar, obviously grateful for the ongoing reprieve from having to entertain their children while they were stranded. Tori's news—and the subsequent visit from a policeman who looked about twelve to confirm that the road would be closed until at least tomorrow—hadn't gone down well with anyone. Well, except maybe the kids, who were having a whale of a time. And Jasper.

He hadn't learned enough about this place

where Tori had grown up to leave just yet. He hadn't learned enough about *Tori*.

She'd disappeared with her Uncle Henry before he'd been able to have a real conversation with her, then hadn't shown herself at all at lunch, while he and Henry had served up sandwiches and home-made sausage rolls. He'd wanted to go and look for her, take her some food, but Henry had shaken his head and kept him downstairs.

That had been hours ago. Now, making paper chains was the only thing that was distracting his curious mind from driving itself mad wondering where Tori was and what she and Henry had talked about.

What was it about her that made him so desperate to *understand*? He'd been happy enough for all of his life so far letting other people exist in their own little bubble, without having to know what made them tick, what mattered to them or why they did the things that they did. So what had changed?

Well. He knew the answer to that well enough. Discovering the truth about his family—that his father had lied to him his whole life, that his best friend had done the same for years—it had cemented the lesson that his first experience of love had taught him at nineteen: no one was really what they seemed. Any happy, smiling facade could conceal a whole barrage of lies. If the people who claimed to care about him most could lie to his face, day after day, how many more deceptions and untruths could people who didn't care about him hide?

But until now that revelation had only made him keep people at arm's length—so far away that they couldn't get close enough for their lies to impact him at all. He'd learned in business to assume that everyone was, at the very least, massaging the facts. And in an industry where most people *were* that caution had served him well.

For some reason, that same assumption had the opposite effect on him when it came to Tori. He wanted to get closer, to draw her in and discover her lies and her secrets.

Maybe it was because they were stuck there, with nothing else to do. Jasper had never been good at boredom. Except he'd found plenty to do, hadn't he, between the kids and the snowmen and the paper chains and helping Henry serve meals?

Maybe it was that night they'd spent together before he left for America. He'd had plenty of other nights with other women, before and since, but something about that one stayed with him. Not the sex—well, not *just* the sex, although that had been pretty damn memorable too—but the feeling of closeness.

To start with it had been drunken conversation and tipsy kisses. Then it had been desperate and lust-driven, glorious sex. But afterwards…that was when things had changed. The alcohol wearing off, and the memory of the papers he'd glimpsed in his father's office coming back to haunt him. Knowing what he had to face the next day, the conversation he had to have. The same frantic feeling of helplessness and concern had started to settle on his chest again—until Tori had stopped it.

Her head resting against his shoulder, she'd run her fingers over his skin and said, 'You're worrying about something. Want to tell me about it, or want me to distract you?'

She'd known, he realised now. Known exactly how it felt to have a worry or a fear that nothing could be done about. How it ate you up and you couldn't stop it.

'Distract me,' he'd said then, and she had.

She'd talked for ages. Not about her past, of course—but about her future. Things she'd hoped for, wanted for herself. Carefully curated ramblings of gentle possibilities, designed to lull him into calm and even sleep. Which, eventually, they had, his heart rate slowing and his muscles relaxing as he sank into her voice and let her warmth soothe him.

There hadn't been any sign of anyone else featuring in her imaginings, Jasper realised with a start, about five years too late. Not him, of course—it had been one night together, she was hardly about to start imagining their future happiness, and he'd have run a mile if she had. But no mention of anyone else, either. Not a shadowy future partner, or kids, or a family at all.

She'd mentioned maybe getting a dog. One day. When she was more settled.

She hadn't, as far as he knew, got one in the five years since.

He glanced at the greyhound by the fire. Had she been remembering the dogs of her childhood when she'd told him that? And was this place the reason she couldn't settle enough to imagine owning a dog, let alone having a family? He suspected it was. And that made his heart ache for her.

Ever since he'd met her, Tori Edwards had been a mystery. But she was one he finally felt on the verge of solving. And for that reason alone, he couldn't be sorry for spending another night here with her, trapped by the snow.

Maybe tonight he'd finally find the answers he craved.

* * *

She was going to have to go back downstairs soon. Lying on her side on her childhood bed, staring out at the falling dusk, Tori knew that she couldn't hide away for ever. As much as she might want to.

'You have to know we don't blame you for what happened to Tyler,' Henry had said that afternoon, his blue eyes sad, the crinkles and wrinkles at the edges making him look older than she'd ever imagined him being.

Eight years she'd been away. Eight birthdays missed, eight Christmases. Eight anniversaries spent standing by a graveside with a bunch of flowers that changed nothing at all.

Of course they blamed her, whatever they said now. And if they didn't, they should. They *would* if they knew the whole story. Even without that knowledge, she remembered the re-criminations in Aunt Liz's eyes the day of the funeral. Remembered how Uncle Henry had barely been able to look at her. Even Flash, the greyhound, had whined and turned away from her.

She'd left the Moorside, left Tyler, for university. And Tyler had died because she was gone.

It was as simple and as awful as that. Of course they blamed her.

The pub itself…that told far more truth than Henry had.

Everything was the same. From Tyler's paintings on the walls, to the menu, to the bar towels hanging in the same old place. It was as if the Moorside had stopped, the day that Tyler died.

She'd tried to make herself go into his bedroom, but failed at the door. Instead, she sat on the floor of the landing, staring at the wooden door, imagining how it looked inside. Because she would bet money it was exactly as she'd left it, eight years ago, the day of the funeral. From the paint on the walls to the faded grey and white chevron blanket Tori's mum had crocheted for him at one of her clubs, to his favourite of his paintings hanging on the wall. The glow-in-the-dark constellations still stuck on the ceiling, and the photo of the two of them on the dresser, with her smiling up at him as if he'd hung the moon, while he beamed at the camera—the kind of young, flawless happiness that people could only experience once in their lives. And once it was broken, there was no way to ever get that innocent joy back again.

Nothing had changed.

It was still her fault that Tyler had died. The only man—boy, really—who'd ever known and loved her.

Now, lying on her own bed again, she forced herself to remember that. To remember the way he'd begged her not to leave him to go to university. How he'd raged about long-distance relationships just being a drawn-out way of breaking up—as if York were the other side of the world. The break in his voice as he'd told her he was scared of what he'd do without her.

And then, six months later, the call from Henry telling her exactly what he *had* done.

'It was an accident, Vicky. He'd had too much to drink, took the bend wrong.'

But she'd known it was more than that. It was what he'd done—what he'd been scared he'd do—without her there to keep him on the rails, keep him safe.

'You're my North Star,' he'd always told her. *'You keep me on the right path.'*

A path he couldn't keep to without her.

He'd died because she hadn't been there to stop it. Henry and Liz *should* blame her.

He was their son. She was just some orphan they took in because she had no one else. And because of decisions she had made, now she had no one at all.

No, that wasn't true. She had *herself*, and that was all she needed. She had an employer, and colleagues. She had a career and purpose and a good income and a home. She'd achieved so much since she'd left this place. There was no point looking back now.

Except for the part where she was actually trapped in her own past.

'Stupid snow,' she muttered as she pushed herself off the bed and onto her feet.

Crossing to the window, she watched the thick flakes falling against the pale glow of the setting sun behind the clouds. Hopefully it would ease off again soon, and maybe tomorrow the road back to the main road at least might be open. She didn't want to go the other way—the Moor Road, past the valley that had claimed Tyler's life—anyway.

Her conversation with Henry buzzed through her mind as she ran a brush through her hair, and splashed her face with water to try and take away some of the blotchiness. The last thing she needed was Jasper asking her why she'd been crying.

Jasper. He seemed to be slipping into life at the inn with astounding speed. Even Henry had commented on how he seemed like a nice young man. Tacit approval for a relationship that didn't exist.

It might have, once, she supposed. That one night they'd spent together…she'd let herself wonder, just for a minute or two, in between the panic, if it might happen again. If it might become something that happened with regularity. Officially, even.

Like a relationship. Not that she wanted or needed such a thing.

But…it had been…nice was the wrong word. But it had been something. Something she hadn't expected to feel again, after Tyler died. A connection. A possibility.

Plus, the sex had been kind of mind-blowing. So much better than her teenage fumblings and experimentation, even if it felt like a betrayal of Tyler to think it.

But then Jasper had left, of course, as she should have known he would. Ever since she'd met him he'd had a parade of girls passing through Flaxstone, none ever staying long enough to make much of an impact. Felix always said it was because he'd been burned by love before, but Tori had her doubts. More likely that Jasper's looks, title and money gave him access to far more adoring women than was good for him, and he didn't even consider that saying no to any of them was a possibility.

She'd thought she had the measure of Jasper, Viscount Darlton, until the evening she'd seen that strange vulnerability in him, and wondered if there might be something more to the man, behind the charm and the confidence. If that one night could have meant something more to him than simply comfort on a bad day.

But then he'd fled the country before she'd even had the chance to stop panicking about having slept with him at all, let alone moved on to actually talking to him about what happened next. Thank God she'd never been stupid enough to fall in love with him. In fact, she'd decided it was probably all for the best, at the time, and that thought had helped her keep that one night firmly at the back of her memory for the last five years. Well, mostly, anyway.

And then he'd come back. He still had that shining brightness he'd had as an entitled, self-confident young man, but there was something more brittle about it now. As if he was trying too hard to be that person again. Tori hadn't been around him enough to even think about why, really, until this week. Or to be reminded of their night together.

But now? Stuck in her childhood home, reliving all the other memories she'd buried for the better part of a decade, and sharing a *bed* with the man?

Yeah. She was thinking about it. She was remembering *everything*.

At least it was more fun than dwelling on Tyler and her many, many mistakes.

With a sigh, Tori decided she was probably about as presentable as she was likely to get, and headed downstairs. Already as she descended she could smell wonderful food scents rising from Henry's kitchen, and wondered what he'd managed to concoct for them for dinner, from whatever he had in the freezers and stores. Having missed lunch, she sincerely hoped it was both hearty and filling. Something to ward off the cold so she didn't feel driven to snuggle quite so close to Jasper tonight.

It would help if he weren't so damn attractive. As much as he could irritate her with that constant bright-side vision, not to mention his entitled, son-of-an-aristocrat presence, she had to admit she sometimes went out of her way to *be* irritated by him. Because if her brain kept telling her how annoying he was, perhaps it would override her body reminding her how damn sexy he was, to boot. That optimist's smile of his was almost impossible not to return, as hard as she tried. And she always knew the instant she failed, because it turned warmer, more heated, as if getting a reaction from her was all just foreplay.

Maybe it was, to him.

Hell, maybe it was to her too.

Because her brain was doing a worse and worse job these days. It had even taken the time to point out how damn cute he was building snowmen with kids, or how non-aristocratic he looked helping Henry dish out dinner last night.

Damn it. She was *not* falling for her boss's son. No way. Not after five years of trying to forget about him.

And definitely not here and now.

But then she walked into the bar and saw Jasper standing on the counter, pinning garishly coloured paper chains to the beams, cheered on by a swarm of grinning children, as Slade blared out of the speakers and she realised that she might already be too late to stop it.

Maybe even five years too late.

Dinner that night was a delicious sort of everything stew that Henry declined to detail the ingredients of, but Jasper suspected was 'everything I could find in the freezer this morning'. He sat perched at the bar mopping his up with a giant hunk of homemade bread, thankful that it was nearly bedtime at least. The one point in the day where Tori couldn't possibly avoid him any longer.

She'd arrived downstairs that evening just as he'd finished decorating the bar, and he'd almost fallen off his stool at the sight of her. Not because she'd changed into some glamorous new outfit, or done anything different with her hair or make-up, like in some high-school romantic-comedy movie. Because she looked so young, so open, and so scared, in a way he'd never seen before.

What the hell did Henry say to her?

Now, an hour or two later, she surprised him all over again—by hoisting herself up onto the bar stool next to him, as Henry placed a pint of bitter in front of her.

'You drink pints?' Jasper asked, figuring she'd probably clam up again if he asked what he really wanted to know. *Are you okay?*

Tori shrugged and took a sip. 'I grew up in a pub. Henry taught me to appreciate the good stuff—whenever Liz wasn't looking.'

Flashing them both a grin, Henry took himself off to serve someone at the far end of the bar.

Jasper hoped the pub was well enough stocked with kids' juices to get them through the night.

'Is it strange, being back here?' That was neutral enough, right? He wasn't asking why she'd left, or what Henry had said that had made her hide herself away all day.

'Very,' Tori said, with feeling. Her eyes cast around the place, as though she was cataloguing everything that had changed in her absence.

'I guess it's a lot different. You said you hadn't been back in eight years...'

She looked up at him sharply. 'When did I say that?'

'When we were talking. Last night.' Damn. He should have known she wouldn't remember; she'd barely been conscious when she said it.

'Right.' She stared down at her pint. 'Well, yes. It's been a while.'

Why? He desperately wanted to know, but he also knew that if he asked she'd never tell him. She was contrary that way. It was one of the things he found most intriguing about her.

'But actually I was just thinking about how everything is exactly the same,' she went on, unprompted. Jasper stayed silent, listening intently. He'd take any scrap of a clue she gave him. 'Same paintings on the walls... It's like a time capsule in here. They've kept everything *exactly* the same. Like they never moved on from—' She broke off.

'You leaving?' Jasper guessed.

Tori gave him a half-amused smile and shook her head. 'No, not that.'

Slipping from his bar stool, Jasper moved from painting to painting, taking in the landscapes and colours, the drama and contrast. He was no great art connoisseur, but he'd spent enough time staring at his ancestors' oil portraits in the Long Gallery at Flaxstone to know he much preferred these slashes of paint that somehow encapsulated the wildness and the wonder of the moors.

'They're great paintings,' he said, returning to his seat. 'And perfect for the location. Why would they change them?'

Her smile was sad, this time. 'They wouldn't. Ever.'

Jasper made a mental note to ask Henry about the paintings.

'So. Are we roomies again tonight?' he asked, bringing the moment back to the present.

'I guess so. It's not like there are suddenly fewer people crammed in here.' Tori didn't sound as if she was jumping with joy at the prospect. Really, she was hell on a guy's ego. But then, just when he was about to say something self-deprecating in the hope of making her laugh—he'd take his wins where he could get them, with her—her expression softened in a way he remembered too well, from one night five years ago. 'You were great with the kids today. I don't know what everyone would have done without you here to keep them entertained.'

Jasper shrugged and looked away. 'I mean, I was pretty bored too. They might have been entertaining me, for all you know.'

She laughed at that, bright and surprised, and he was glad she didn't know the truth. That kids were easier for him to interact with because they'd had less time to build up all the secrets and lies.

Maybe that was the real reason he wanted to solve the puzzle of Tori Edwards. If he knew all her secrets, maybe he could let her in, for real, and tell her his. If Felix hadn't already.

Maybe they could have that one night again. And maybe he could get back that feeling he'd had when he was with her. Soothed and relaxed and hopeful. As if the world was shining with possibilities, not tarred and dull with lies and deception.

Maybe if one person, this person, gave up their secrets voluntarily, he could have faith again. Faith that some people could live without secrets, or without deceptions meant to hurt others or protect themselves.

Jasper knew, suddenly, somehow, that if he ever had faith in anyone, it would be Tori Edwards.

And he wanted it so much that it hurt.

CHAPTER SIX

TORI STARED AT the single bed. Somehow, it looked even smaller than it had last night.

'Do you want me to sleep on the floor tonight?' Jasper asked, obviously catching her studious observations of their sleeping place. 'I mean, I *probably* won't freeze to death. Much. And even if I did, I don't reckon my dad would fire you.'

Rolling her eyes, Tori yanked back the covers. 'But after today, Henry and Liz would never forgive me, and I'd have seven kids after my blood if you weren't around to throw snowballs at tomorrow.'

'True.' Jasper flashed her a smug smile. It really shouldn't be as attractive as it was. 'I am easy to love.'

Did she imagine it, or was there a brittleness to his words? As if there might actually be some vulnerability behind the bravado and self-confidence. Something she'd never even really looked for until now.

Tori shook her head. It seemed unlikely.

But then, so did Viscount Darlton sitting on the floor of the Moorside Inn making paper chains with children.

They prepared for bed in silence—at least, *they* were quiet. In the absence of conversation Tori could hear the whole inn settling down for the night. Kids protesting bedtime; adults laughing over one last pint; the faint strains of Christmas hits from yesteryear still playing through the ancient speakers. Downstairs, Henry would be wiping down the bar, and Liz would be fetching the keys, ready to lock up. No need to shoo out the last of the patrons tonight; with the snow still thick on the ground, no one was leaving.

How many nights had she hidden in the shadows on the stairs, watching Henry and Liz put the pub to bed? Feeling so safe, so loved, here at the Moorside?

But that was a long time ago. Before Tyler.

'What are you thinking so hard about?' Jasper asked, softly, as she climbed into the bed beside him.

'Tyler,' she whispered back, without even thinking about what she was saying.

He stilled behind her. 'Henry told me that the paintings we talked about earlier were painted by their son, Tyler. The same one, I assume?'

Tori nodded. She didn't trust herself to answer. But she had nowhere to go and nowhere to hide from this conversation now she'd started it. And maybe she'd spent too many years not talking about Tyler anyway.

Maybe Jasper would understand. Not if she told him everything, of course—then he'd just know the truth. He'd know that Tyler's death was her fault, the same way Henry and Liz knew it, and then she'd never be able to look him in the eye again.

And Jasper had nice eyes. Despite herself, she couldn't deny she liked looking at them. At him.

He touched her shoulder, and she turned to face him. She could barely make out his features in the darkness and the moonlight, but she knew his face well enough to picture it through the gloom. Knew his body too, even after only one night. One night she'd spent a lot of years pretending to forget.

She hadn't forgotten any of it.

'You and Tyler were…together?' Jasper asked. There was a twist of his mouth, even in the dark, that Tori knew was distaste for the idea. Maybe even jealousy.

Something about that warmed her, even though she hated herself for it. There was no point being jealous of a dead man, after all.

'Ever since I was sixteen,' she said. 'Henry and Liz weren't thrilled about it, but…it wasn't like we'd ever been brought up as brother or sister or anything, and we weren't actually related, so there wasn't much they could do. Well, except for Henry's epic "not under my roof" talks.'

'Which I'm sure you ignored.'

'Not for the first year or two,' Tori admitted. 'Although we did decide that the barns at the far edge of the pub lands didn't really count as his roof.'

It had been so exciting, sneaking off together, honestly believing that no one else knew where they were going or what they were doing—although as an adult, Tori realised that they probably all had. No one who had watched them together could have seen anything but young, first love. The infatuated kind. The kind that blinded a person to the whole rest of the world.

Until it didn't, any more.

'So, what happened?' Jasper asked. 'Where is Tyler now?'

Tori shut her eyes. 'He died. While I was away at university.'

She heard his sharp intake of breath, felt the pity in his gaze even if she couldn't see it. His fingers twitched against her hip as if he wanted to hold her close, to take away the pain.

But the pain was eight years old now. Dull and aching like an old injury that only hurt when it snowed. Tyler was with her every minute of every day, a ghost looking over her shoulder.

But if she didn't turn around, didn't look back, at least she didn't have to see the accusation in his eyes. The hate and the blame.

'I'm so sorry,' Jasper said, after a long time.

'Yeah.'

Because what else was there to say? Other than, *It was my fault. I killed him the day I went away.*

Tori turned to face away from him again, holding her hurt tight inside, even when all she really wanted to do was curl into Jasper's body and let him hold her while she cried.

She didn't deserve the tears. Not when she was to blame.

So instead, she tried to sleep. Even though she knew that Tyler would be waiting in her dreams.

He always was on nights like this.

That was what she deserved tonight.

* * *

Jasper woke suddenly, unsure of what had disturbed him. He'd been luxuriating in a particularly relaxing dream—one so opposite to his actual life he'd known even as he experienced it that it couldn't be real. In it, he and Tori were walking beside a frozen river, gloved hands clasped together. He looked up to see the strange battlements of Stonebury Hall rising against the winter sky ahead of them, snow coating them like icing sugar on one of Felix's mother's cakes.

They didn't talk at all—which was probably just as well, as an argument would have ruined the perfect peace of the dream—but Jasper knew he was happy, content, in a way he didn't remember being since he'd discovered the truth about his father and his half-brother.

Of course, it couldn't last.

Jasper blinked into the darkness, trying to put his finger on what had jerked him out of the dream and wondering if he could get back to it if he fell asleep again quickly enough. But then Tori cried out—a sound of such pain and torment it twisted his heart—and he knew that he wasn't going to be sleeping again any time soon.

'Tori? Tori.' He pressed a hand to her shoulder, feeling the heat of her skin burning through her T-shirt despite the chill in the air. 'Wake up.'

She didn't, though. Instead, she sobbed again, and buried her face in his chest, crying in a way he'd never even imagined Victoria Edwards was capable of.

All those battlements were broken, the mask cast aside and the brittle shield she kept up, always, shattered.

Jasper knew she'd never have let him see her this way under any other circumstances. He was pretty sure that the moment it was over Tori would pretend that it had never happened. He couldn't blame her; he wouldn't want her—or anyone—to see him so broken, either. To see deep inside him where the pain lived. Hell, he'd moved continents to avoid it. Staying at Flaxstone with his father and Felix would have made that hurt raw and visible every day—and so he'd left, and only returned when he knew his defences were strong enough to hide it.

But now, holding Tori, he wondered if *any* emotional defences were strong enough to hide behind, in the end. Maybe everything always came out, eventually. Just like secrets and truths.

'Tori, sweetheart.' He whispered the words

against her hair, kissing her head softly as her cries lessened. 'Wake up, love.'

And she did.

Lifting her head, she blinked up at him, tears still glistening in the half-light. 'I was dreaming…' She shuddered at the memory.

'About Tyler?' he asked gently. She nodded. 'Would it help to talk about it?'

This time, she shook her head, her hair whipping around in defiance. 'I just want to forget.' She looked up at him again, and there were no tears his time. Just a new fierceness to replac the armour she'd lost. Her body shifted, ad suddenly every inch of her seemed to be essed up against him, tempting and hot an everything he'd never even dreamed of.

That was a liHe'd dreamed about it. *Often.* Especially sir the night they'd spent together.

But he'd ne imagined it could actually happen ag ain,t here and now.

She rais ed lmouth, pressing it firmly to his, her tor gweeping out across his lower lip, and his w body shuddered with want and desire as issed her back. The kiss was deep and d spe and everything he ren 2e bered abou t tother night together. V she pulled bjust far enough to k way along his jawline, Jasper could barely remember his own name.

'Help me forget?' she murmured against his ear.

And suddenly the heat faded.

Not completely, of course. The lust she'd inspired was still coursing through his blood, and certain parts of his anatomy were *absolutely* on board with her plan—right now, preferably.

But his brain, that frustrating, overthinking part of him—the part that had come up with a dream of a frozen river and his woman's hand in his—had other ideas.

'Tori...' He pulled away as far as he could without falling out of the narrow single bed. 'Tori, not like this.'

God, he wanted her. She wanted her to want *him*, too. Not just forgetfulness, not just oblivion. He'd had enough that sort of relationship himself, when he first moved away from Flaxstone. The kind of sex that just blocked out the world for time, that helped him pass out and sleep out dreaming of the life he'd thought he'd and the lies that backed behind it.

He didn't want that with her. Not this time. The same had been free—for him, at least. It'd just helped to forget his worries, she'd given him new hope for what came next. Hope that had only lasted until the next day, when he'd confronted his father, but still. It hadn't been despair or desperation that had driven him to her, not like it was for her now. Now he wondered again what it had been for Tori that had allowed her to let him in that night.

Whatever that was, he knew that if they were to have that connection again, he needed it to be something more. *Tori* meant something more to him, now. Seeing her at the Moorside these last couple of days had convinced him of that, if nothing else.

She mattered. It might not be love or for ever or any of the other impossible things his dream had seemed to promise him. But it was more than this—more than forgetting who she was in his body for a while.

And he knew, if he took what she was offering right now, he'd never be worthy of anything more.

'Tori. Tori, no. Not like this.' He said it again as gently as he could, but hurt flashed across her face all the same. He was so close he could see it, pale in the moonlight.

But then she nodded in acceptance. 'I know. I just…it still hurts.'

'I imagine it always will.' He didn't know about this sort of emotional pain, not really.

But he understood about having a whole world he thought he knew being snatched away from him.

What sort of a future had Tori imagined with Tyler? How much must she have loved him to have not even been able to come back and see her family because the pain was so great?

Jasper wasn't foolish enough to imagine she might ever love *him* that way—wasn't even sure he'd know what to do with that kind of love if she did. But just for a moment, in the darkness, he wondered how it would feel. To be loved *so much*.

Had his father loved Felix's mother that way? Did his own mother love his father enough that she'd love him still when the truth came out?

He didn't know. He'd run away before he could ask those questions.

But suddenly, holding a silent Tori in his arms, he wondered.

How had they loved each other? And could he forgive them, if it was enough?

Maybe, with the thaw, it would be time to find out.

Tori woke alone, this time. Hardly surprising, given the way she'd behaved the night before. She cringed even to remember it.

But Jasper hadn't mocked her, hadn't been smug or even dismissive. He hadn't even said just *no*.

He'd said, *'No, not like this.'*

And he'd been right.

Of course, the odds were good he'd tease and joke about it this morning, make comments about his ego and her flattery of it being good for the soul or something. But the more time she spent with him on this abortive road trip, the more she came to realise that those jibes and barbs weren't the real Jasper. They were the thorns and brambles he used to keep people away. To stop them from seeing the man inside.

But she'd seen him. Well, glimpsed him, at least. Watching him with the children, or helping Henry. Feeling his arms around her as she cried. And the strain in his voice as he told her no, more telling than his words of how much he was giving up.

She'd felt the real Jasper in his kiss. And she knew for certain now that he was nothing like the entitled, shallow man he pretended to be.

Tori wasn't entirely sure what to do with this information just yet.

Make fun of him, probably. Wasn't that the way their relationship went?

But maybe it didn't have to, any more.

She was still thinking about the possibilities as she headed downstairs thirty minutes later, washed and dressed and as presentable as she was going to get while wearing the same clothes she'd had on for three days now. Not that it could matter all that much; Jasper had seen her at her worst last night, in the grips of a nightmare and covered in sweat, and he'd still wanted her. And Liz and Henry…well, they'd seen her in her teenage Goth phase, so nothing would alarm them now.

Jasper was perched at the bar when she walked in, surprised to find the place less busy than it had been yesterday. Across in the dining room she could see people folding sheets and packing bags through the open doorway.

'The roads are open?' she guessed.

Jasper nodded. 'Well, the way back to the main road is open. The moors road is still closed, so we'll have to go the long way round. But when you're ready we can head out and go…home.'

There was a slight pause before the last word, as if he realised that Flaxstone could never really be her home, not while the Moorside still stood, not even if she never came back here ever again. She'd had home once.

She didn't expect to be so lucky as to find it twice.

Except maybe he was thinking of his own complicated feelings about the place. Tori didn't know what had driven him away from Flaxstone, or what had persuaded him to return, but she knew he hadn't seemed at ease on the estate ever since he'd arrived back in the country.

The time they'd spent at the Moorside Inn might not have been planned, or convenient, or even what she'd have chosen if she'd had any say in the matter at all. But Tori had to admit that it had changed them. It had given them the space to see deeper into each other, behind their defences.

And it had given *her* the chance to be part of a family again.

Walking away from that a second time somehow felt far, far harder than it had been eight years ago, deep in the grip of her grief and guilt over Tyler's death.

'You'll come back and see us soon, won't you, Vicky?' Aunt Liz said, holding her hands tight as Jasper loaded their stuff into the car. They seemed to be leaving with more than they'd arrived with—including two of Uncle Henry's steak and ale pies from the freezer, something that had made Jasper beam. There was something else, too—something wrapped in Christmas paper, that she hadn't been allowed to examine too closely. Tori was fine with that. Christmas presents smacked too much of family, and togetherness, and all the things she needed to say goodbye to again.

She wasn't 'Vicky' any longer. She'd been Tori since the day she walked out. Vicky and her dreams and ambition and selfishness had got Tyler killed. And even that hadn't been enough for her to give them up entirely.

She didn't want to be Vicky again. It hurt too much.

But Aunt Liz looked so hopeful, her grip on Tori's hands so desperate, that she couldn't tell her that. 'Sure. I'll come soon.'

'For Christmas maybe?' Aunt Liz pressed.

'Maybe.' Tori gave a faint smile, and pressed a kiss to Liz's cheek. Her skin felt more papery, older than Tori remembered.

They were all older now. Just not necessarily wiser.

'We'll look forward to it,' Henry said, leaning in for his own hug and kiss. 'Family shouldn't be apart at Christmas.'

Jasper came over to make his last goodbyes and then, suddenly, they were back on the road again.

SOPHIE PEMBROKE 113

Tori watched the Moorside Inn grow smaller and smaller in the wing mirror, and blinked away more tears she refused to shed when it disappeared completely.

CHAPTER SEVEN

SNOW STILL COVERED the land around them, inches deep and untouched except for the odd footprint or animal track. The road, however, was that horrible grey mush of snow mixed with salt and earth, churned up by car tyres. Jasper took the drive slowly, carefully, wondering if maybe they should have at least waited until after lunch to set out. But as soon as she'd heard the road was open, Tori had been getting ready to leave and shoving his backpack and laptop towards him.

The Moorside Inn might have been her home once, but she'd been conspicuously eager to leave it.

The memory of Tyler, he supposed, remembering that strange, middle-of-the-night connection between them after her dream. She hadn't mentioned it this morning, unsurprisingly, so neither had he. In fact, she hadn't mentioned much at all, and they'd reached the main road in complete silence. Jasper was starting to think they'd be all the way home at Flaxstone before Tori spoke, if then.

But they couldn't just go back to being the people they'd been before they got snowed in together, could they?

Then, she'd been a challenge to him—and he was pretty sure he'd just been an annoyance to her. They had the memory of their one night together, sure, but that had been five long years ago. They'd both changed since then, right? He knew for certain that he had.

And he'd changed again over the last few days. No, not him, exactly. But his understanding of who Tori was, and his strange compulsion to know her better. He couldn't return to being just colleagues—and acrimonious ones at that.

He wanted more.

He wanted her in his bed again tonight—a bed with enough room to spread out so that when she slept snuggled in his arms he knew it was because she wanted to be there, not just to avoid falling onto the hard floor.

And he wanted her wide awake, not dreaming. Wanted her thinking of him, not a dead lover he could never compete with.

Jasper shook his head and refocussed his attention on the road. What was he doing? Imagining himself in competition with the memory of an eighteen-year-old boy he'd never met?

Tori wasn't his girlfriend, or even his lover. She was barely even a friend.

But somehow, the last few days, she'd seemed so much more.

At the Moorside, in their snow-induced bubble of time, she'd seemed like a partner. Maybe family, even. At the bare minimum, a real friend. One he badly wanted to kiss...

Would he be able to cling onto that seed of a relationship, once they were back at Flaxstone? It felt as if the connection between them were a tiny seedling, poking its head through the snow too early, and the slightest frost could kill it off.

But Jasper was determined to nurture it and help it grow. He'd seen behind Tori's defences now, and he wanted that woman in his life. Not the brittle, argumentative, sarcastic woman he'd seen since he'd returned—well, actually, he wanted her too. He wanted all of her.

Hell. He really was in trouble.

By the time they pulled into Flaxstone Hall it was early afternoon, and Jasper's eyes ached from focussing on the treacherous roads and idiots who didn't know how to drive in the snow. The last thing he wanted to do was deal

with his family, especially his father. But Tori
had other ideas.

'We should go and check in with the earl
and give him our report from Stonebury,' she
announced, before he'd even cut the engine.

'Now?' he asked plaintively, as he climbed
out of the car. 'Can't we just go back to bed
first?'

She arched an eyebrow at him. 'Together?'

'Well, preferably,' he admitted.

With a sigh, Tori opened her own door, got
out, and moved to meet him in front of the
bonnet. 'Jasper, do you want my list of reasons
why that would be a bad idea alphabetically or
in order of importance?'

Ouch. 'Why don't you just give me the top
three?' Hopefully ones he could counter with
a reminder of just how good they could be
in bed together. That searing kiss the night
before had definitely confirmed for him that
five years hadn't stolen any of the passion that
they'd shared.

But Tori lifted her hands to tick her points
off on her fingers. 'One, we need to talk to
your father—like we were supposed to two
days ago. He doesn't like waiting. Two, I've
been wearing these clothes for three days and
I'm exhausted. And three, you and I both know
that you'll be running back off to the States

again soon, and I'm not all that interested in being another of the background models in your peacock strut across the estate, thanks.'

'My peacock strut?' He didn't have a strut. But he was pretty sure that number three was the only reason that was really stopping Tori after last night.

'You definitely do. I had the misfortune to witness it for years with every new girl you brought home.' She sighed. 'Look, Jasper, I'm sorry if I gave you the wrong idea last night. I was…upset. But I honestly believe that…giving in to anything between us again would be a bad idea. We were just caught up in the romance of being stranded in the snow.'

'With about thirty other people,' Jasper observed.

What was he missing here? She wouldn't quite look him in the eye, he realised, and her hands were clasped tightly in front of her. Upset or not, he knew that the *attraction* had been real between them last night, which meant that her reasons not to act on it must be stronger.

Was this really because he'd had plenty of girlfriends in the past? Or because she knew he was leaving soon and didn't want a meaningless fling? Both perfectly good reasons, except…they hinted at her wanting some-thing *more*.

Jasper felt suddenly warm inside, despite the icy air all around them.

He'd avoided even a *hint* of more for years. But with Tori…maybe it wasn't impossible?

Or maybe she wasn't giving him the whole reason for her reluctance. Was this to do with *his* romantic past—or *hers*?

Eight years since Tyler died and she still woke up screaming from nightmares of losing him. Maybe *he* was the real reason she wasn't willing to move on, if she knew that what was between them was more than just a fling.

And now his head was starting to hurt with all the possibilities.

Rolling his eyes, he felt his usual arrogant, aristocratic demeanour taking over, the way it always did when he was confused or threat-ened or embarrassed. It was an automatic de-fence system, just like Tori's, he supposed, if a little flimsier.

'Fine, you don't want to go to bed with me. But I still think bed should be top of our list of priorities today. I'd happily take going to bed solo over dealing with dear old Dad right now.' In truth, he wanted a little more time to marshal his arguments for making Stone-bury an escape for his mother. He *should* have been planning that while he'd been stuck at the Moorside, but he'd been a little...distracted. 'All that entertaining kids and serving meals wears a guy out, you know.'

'Should have known you couldn't handle an honest day's work,' Tori responded tartly.

Neither of them mentioned again the lack of sleep they'd suffered the night before after her nightmares, or the staying up late sharing secrets. Tori had packed that back in its box with her vague apology for 'giving him the wrong idea'. Already, Flaxstone had brought back the people they'd been before the Moorside Inn. He should have expected it, but it hurt all the same.

'Really, though. Can't reporting in wait until tomorrow? Or at least later this afternoon?'

Tori opened the car door and stepped out into the snow. 'Time and earl wait for no man.'

Then she strode towards the imposing doors of the place Jasper used to call home, and he found himself following without deciding to.

Until he doubled back, rescued the steak and ale pies from the boot, and decided to detour past the kitchens to pop them in the fridge for later. See? Totally in control of his own life, really.

They found the earl in his study—well, once they'd stopped by the kitchens. Even Tori couldn't argue with the fact that Henry's pies took priority over almost everything else.

Especially over any more discussion of what had happened between them last night.

She'd been brutally honest with her three reasons for Jasper, but she couldn't deny that she'd held one of them back.

I can't risk falling for you when I know you're leaving.

Already, he felt like someone new. Or rather, someone she'd hoped existed—the Jasper from the night they'd spent together. Maybe that Jasper really was there, underneath all the charm and the confidence. But she couldn't risk letting him out—or letting him into her heart. Even if he drastically changed his playboy ways—which she doubted—he'd be going back to the States after Christmas. And Tori knew better than anyone that long-distance relationships were a tragedy waiting to happen—or at the very least a disaster.

When he'd left last time, she'd been fine, because despite her hopes she'd still known who he was. It hadn't been a surprise that one night together was all they'd had. Leaving the country had seemed a little extreme, but whatever. Her heart had been safe.

This time...this time, he kept making paper chains and helping Uncle Henry and holding her when she cried and it was all far too much. This time, if she let herself fall any further... she feared for her heart when he went away again.

She'd spent eight years protecting her heart—from the hatred Liz and Henry would feel towards her if they knew everything about Tyler's death, from the guilt she felt herself, and from anyone else who might try and damage it even further. She wasn't about to stop now.

Which meant that focussing on work again for the rest of Jasper's visit was by far the best possible plan.

The earl looked up from the papers on his desk and studied them both with that strange, scrutinising stare he'd given Tori the first day they'd met. As if he were in the audience, watching her on the stage, waiting to see what she'd do next. An observer, not involved in her life choices.

How strange that he'd look at his son the same way, she realised suddenly. Jasper must have had his reasons for leaving, after all. She'd just never managed to ask him about them.

The Earl of Flaxstone had been Tori's benefactor since she was eighteen years old. It was a ridiculously old-fashioned term, but then, the earl was an old-fashioned kind of guy, and in the years since Tori had never been able to find a word that better described their relationship.

He'd discovered her not long before she'd left for university, when he'd stopped by the Moorside Inn. She'd been sitting outside at one of the picnic tables, studying the inn's books, trying to find somewhere to save some money. Times and takings had been lean just then, and Henry and Liz had needed any help they could get—but Tori just hadn't known enough to be any help at all.

She'd said as much to the earl, when he'd stopped by to ask what she was doing. She hadn't known who he was then, of course, but her frustration had leaked out all the same. When she'd looked up to see exactly who she was talking to, she'd seen the same considering look on his face as she saw now. As if he was deciding quite what to do with her.

Last time, he'd offered a few suggestions—negotiating down the cost of some of their overheads, and other obvious things that she would have known if she hadn't been eighteen and ignorant—then given her his card, with instructions to look him up if ever she needed a job.

She'd left for university a month later, and it had only been the following spring, after Tyler's death, that she'd dug out the card, steeled herself, and called him. After all, by then, she'd known she couldn't go home again. So she'd do whatever it took to find somewhere else to go.

It had been a good call. The earl had given her more than a place to go. He'd given her holiday work on the estate that summer—and all the holidays after that, which suited her perfectly. He'd offered advice and insight when she'd been deciding her course of study in her second and third years. Then, once she graduated—top of her business class—he'd offered her a better-paying and more interesting job than any of the other companies she'd interviewed for, and accommodation to boot. And not the staff dormitories, filled with sweaty students all summer, and freezing cold in the winter. Her own little cottage on the edge of the estate, to live in as she pleased.

She'd repaid his confidence in her, she thought, working her way up to become his trusted lieutenant, learning everything she could about the estate's business and developing it further every year. The earl hadn't exactly been a father figure to her, but he'd been a great boss, and she knew she would always owe him for the opportunities he'd given her.

Which was why she felt so damn awkward with him staring at her and Jasper this way.

'So. You've returned from your little adventure, then?' he asked, his gaze still flitting between the two of them. 'Felix filled me in.'

'More an inconvenience than an adventure,' Tori replied, taking her usual seat opposite him as he indicated she should. Jasper stayed standing, ignoring the chair at his own side, and his father's gesture to sit.

Obstinate man.

It hadn't escaped Tori's notice that Jasper seemed reluctant to spend any time at all with his father. In fact, she couldn't remember even seeing them together since he'd returned. Before he'd left, she'd have always said they were quite close. Clearly something fundamental had changed.

Apparently she wasn't the only one keeping family secrets.

'I'd have emailed our initial report on Stonebury Hall to you,' Tori went on, when it became obvious that Jasper had nothing to add to the conversation, 'but the Internet connection at the Moorside has always been spotty.' He was lucky she'd even managed to get a text message out to warn him they'd been delayed. Her call to Felix had only gone through when she was out by the road. Inside the inn calls were practically impossible. She'd seen plenty of the other guests standing up on the snow-covered picnic tables trying to get a signal.

The earl's attention was all on her now, as if Jasper weren't even in the room. 'And how was the old homestead?' he asked casually.

Tori hesitated before answering. She'd never told the earl her reasons for leaving, or for not returning. But now she wondered how much he knew. The Moorside wasn't *that* far from Flaxstone, and who was to say the earl hadn't stopped by there once or twice in the last few years? It was where she'd *met* him, after all. Why had that never occurred to her before?

'It was…fine. A little crowded. There were a number of families taking shelter there. Jasper entertained the kids,' she added, throwing him a smile.

He didn't return it. Neither did the earl.

Right. Maybe it was better to just concentrate on business for a while.

'So, uh, Stonebury Hall.' She handed over her tablet with the photos she'd taken of their visit for the earl to look through while she talked. 'It wasn't quite as spacious as we were hoping, or perhaps that space just isn't being used very well—I think the floor plans and photos from the agent were a little misleading. But there's definite potential for a farm shop and café-style business, and I could see the outbuildings being used for craft stalls, or maybe even a children's soft-play area.'

'I disagree,' Jasper said suddenly. 'It's far too small a property, battlements or not. It would be best used as a home. Perhaps even a family bolthole or escape, should anyone need it.' He stared hard at his father as he spoke, while Tori gave him her own, incredulous stare. Then the pieces started to fall into place.

Of course he wanted to keep the place for himself, the entitled, selfish prat. Had she really thought she'd seen another side to him while they were at the inn? How foolish of her. At heart he was just what he'd always been. A spoilt little rich boy who thought he deserved everything and ran away when he didn't get it.

Thank God she hadn't given in to him.

'I think Stonebury has far greater potential than just another holiday cottage,' she argued. 'The rental on such a place, probably only in season, would be far lower than if we put the whole property to work. Not to mention that *my* plan would make the land and the house available to local people—*all* of them, not just those who could afford to hire the place.'

The earl might be a quintessential aristocrat, with more land and money than anyone had any reason to expect in this world, but he'd always been enthusiastic about sharing it—to a point. The estate lands were generally open to walkers and locals, and they ran many events at the hall and gardens, as well as on the wider lands, throughout the year. Partly, Tori knew, that had begun as a way to keep the estate profitable after his father had almost run it into the ground. But with the earl's hard work, and her help over the last few years, the Flaxstone estate and business interests were more than profitable enough that he could have closed up the metaphorical drawbridge and kept Flaxstone private again. Instead, he'd begun using it for more charitable endeavours instead of paying ones, allowing even more people to make use of the estate.

She'd asked him once why he chose to run things that way. He'd responded that the estates were a part of history, one that belonged to the whole of the British Isles. He was merely their custodian for a time.

She liked that. She liked him. And the idea that his only son and heir was trying to take the whole family and estate backwards annoyed the hell out of her.

Jasper shot her a glare. 'Perhaps this is something we can discuss in private. *Father.*' The emphasis was obvious, an attempt to stake a higher claim on their boss's attention. And it made Tori's blood boil.

To think she'd been starting to actually *like* the guy. Had confided in him. Found comfort in him.

Kissed him.

Grabbing her tablet and notes, she gave the earl a quick nod. 'By all means. I wouldn't want to come between *family*.'

And then she walked out of the office before she threw something at the Viscount Darlton's far too gorgeous head.

'Well. I think you've got some making up to do there,' Jasper's father said as they both watched Tori stalk out of the office. 'I *was* hoping that some time away together would help you two find some common ground, build a friendship perhaps, but…' He sighed. 'So. Tell me why you think Tori is wrong about Stonebury Hall.'

An uncomfortable feeling settled in Jasper's stomach. 'I don't think she's *wrong* exactly.' But that was what it had sounded like, he realised now. No wonder Tori had stormed off. 'Stonebury *could* be all the things she thinks it could. But at its heart, that house is a home—and I know she felt it too. But she's thinking about your property empire and her job. I'm thinking about our family. And *your* plans to ruin us.'

There was an echo of that desperate, clenching, wrenching feeling in his chest—the same one he'd felt when he'd first read his father's email, thousands of miles and a few weeks away from there.

It's time to be upfront and honest with the world. Felix deserves my acknowledgement as my son.

No consideration about what Jasper deserved and—more importantly—no thought of how it would affect his mother, the earl's dutiful Lady Flaxstone for almost thirty years. His father was just doing whatever *he* thought was best, or simply whatever he wanted. Just as he'd done when he'd had an affair with Felix's mother while engaged to Jasper's.

Other people were the last thing the Earl of Flaxstone thought about.

The earl sighed again. 'You're still against me publicly acknowledging Felix as my son.'

'Yes! Of course I am!'

'I never realised the Flaxstone reputation mattered so much to you, Jasper. I would have thought, if you were so concerned about our legacy and your place in it, you might have stayed to help protect it personally.' There was an edge to his father's words now. One a younger Jasper would have swerved away from, made nice to avoid that sharpness of the earl's temper.

But Jasper wasn't a child any longer. He knew his own mind. And he knew when his father was just plain wrong.

'I am deeply concerned about my mother's well-being. I can't stop you doing this—God knows, no one ever stopped you doing anything you wanted—but if you insist on making our private lives public then at least give Mother somewhere to take solace and refuge from the media chaos that will follow. Buy Stonebury, let her retire there until everything blows over.' Jasper remembered those incongruous battlements and crenellations. That was what she needed. Protection. Defences. She'd never really had any of her own, and so Jasper would have to give her some.

'If there's any decency left in you, don't drag her down with you,' he said. Then he turned and walked out on his father, pushing past Felix as he appeared in the doorway.

'Jasper?' his one-time best friend said, but Jasper ignored him.

Felix's paternity wasn't his fault—Jasper knew that logically. But hiding the truth from him for so many years was. Felix had known the truth ever since his mother died, years before, and not told him. Jasper wasn't ready to forgive that just yet. Not until he knew that his mother was protected.

At least he'd given his father something to think about. And now…now he was rather afraid he had to find Tori and explain himself. Maybe even apologise.

He pulled a face, even though there was no one to see it. He hated apologising.

Perhaps he'd make a stop for one of Henry's pies, first. For the energy. After all, he'd asked Mrs Rawkins, the cook, to put one on to warm for him before they went to meet his father. It would be a shame for it to go to waste, and Tori would probably take a little time to calm down, anyway.

He veered left, down the corridor that led to the kitchens, and took a moment to appreciate the aroma of steak and ale pie, wafting towards him. Yes, this was definitely the right decision.

Then he walked in, and saw Tori lifting a forkful of *his* pie to *her* mouth. He froze. She gave him a wicked grin, then ate the mouthful right in front of him.

'Mmm…' she said, licking her lips. 'Delicious. Shame there's hardly any left.'

'Henry gave us two pies.' Jasper shot an accusing look at Mrs Rawkins, who folded her arms across her ample chest.

'Don't you give me that look. Tori told me everything.' Sadly, Mrs Rawkins had known him for his whole life, and any respect she'd had for his title or station had long since faded away in a litany of stolen food, broken plates, and his and Felix's teenage attempts to fix themselves food when returning late from the pub.

'What, exactly, did she tell you?' Jasper asked. And when had Tori got Mrs Rawkins on her side anyway? He shook his head. 'Never mind, I can imagine.' Probably the truth as she saw it, embellished to make him out to be as evil as possible.

Tori deserved to know the real truth—about his family, his father, his half-brother, and why he was acting the way he was. She was stuck in the middle of it all, another pawn in his father's game, and he owed her the full story, however hard it was to tell it.

But more than that, he *wanted* her to know. Because he couldn't bear her looking at him again the way she had when they were in his father's office. Not when she'd finally started to look at him differently, while they were away.

And who knew? Maybe it would even do

him some good to have someone to talk to about the whole sordid affair. Although, if his father got his way, soon he'd be able to discuss it with the whole world.

The thought didn't cheer him at all.

He looked at Tori, who was happily cutting herself another piece of pie. 'I don't suppose you're going to share that, are you?'

Tori shook her head as she chewed another mouthful, her expression blissful. 'Nope. But, like you say, there's another one.'

'In the freezer,' Mrs Rawkins added. 'Take hours to cook now, that will.'

Jasper sighed, and sank into the chair opposite Tori to watch her eat his pie.

'Fine,' he said. 'Consider me punished. But when you're finished, perhaps you'll do me the courtesy of letting me explain myself.'

Tori's eyebrow's shot up in obvious surprise. 'Okay,' she said, after a moment of chewing. 'When I'm done.'

'Great.' Jasper sank back in his chair and prepared to endure his punishment.

CHAPTER EIGHT

HENRY'S PIES WERE always delicious, but watching Jasper's pained expression as she ate it in front of him made the whole dining experience even more sublime for Tori.

Eventually, she set her cutlery down on her empty plate, thanked Mrs Rawkins—who had been a dear ally ever since she'd discovered that Tori knew her way around a kitchen and could be a big help when there was an event on and not enough trained hands on deck—and turned to Jasper, her arms folded across her middle.

'Okay. Explain.'

And it had better be something more convincing than, *I'm a poor little rich boy who always got everything I want so I don't know any better.*

'Not here.' Jasper's gaze darted around the kitchen furtively, as if he thought Mrs Rawkins might intervene or take sides—which she'd totally already done, so it seemed a bit pointless. 'Let's go take a walk by the river.'

'Yay. More snow and ice,' Tori replied, letting the sarcasm flow. But, actually, the kitchens were warm and stuffy, and she could do with walking off some of that pie before she fell into a food coma, so she followed him all the same.

They paused in the boot room to grab hats, gloves, scarves, warm coats and walking boots—all the things Tori wished they'd had with them when they were stranded on the moors. Maybe then they could have escaped to somewhere other than the Moorside Inn. *Anywhere* else would have been ideal.

Not just because of having to see Aunt Liz and Uncle Henry again. If she was honest, having that time with them had been kind of… lovely. Her guilt still sat heavy in her chest, too easily revived by being back in that place where her romance with Tyler had flourished and died. But feeling part of a family again? That part she'd enjoyed.

No, the reason she so bitterly regretted their pit stop in her past was walking beside her, as they strode out from the manor and towards the river that ran along the edge of the woods on the far side of the estate.

Spending time with Jasper had helped her

see him in a new light. A more hopeful one. She'd got to know a man she'd thought she could actually *like*. Maybe even care for.

But the minute they'd returned to Flaxstone he'd reverted to type. People didn't really change—she knew that. And trying to make someone into something they weren't never ended well. She'd learnt that with Tyler. Or maybe he'd learnt it from her—the very hard way.

Jasper was what he was: a spoilt only child who went through women as she went through chocolate, and who hadn't ever learned to think about anybody but himself.

'I want to explain exactly what was going on in my father's study earlier,' Jasper said as the river came into view.

'Besides you being a Grade-A tosser?' Tori asked cheerfully. He shot her a glare, and she added, 'If you want to change my mind about that, you really should have started with an apology.'

Jasper sighed. He looked exhausted, she realised suddenly. Probably at least partly because she'd kept him up half the night with her nightmares.

Maybe she owed him a little bit of an apology too. But not unless he said sorry first.

'I apologise,' Jasper said stiffly. He seemed

nothing like the joking, carefree guy she'd known when she'd first started at Flaxstone, or the irritating, sarcastic one he'd been since his return. And he definitely wasn't the relaxed, smiling man who'd built snowmen and paper chains with kids at the Moorside. Was she missing something? What exactly was going on here? 'I shouldn't have dismissed your ideas in front of my father like that.'

'So why did you?' Tori asked, feeling an echo of the hurt she'd felt back in the office. But the look of pain that flashed across Jasper's face was far more intense. And intriguing. 'Did you honestly not agree with me?'

'It wasn't that exactly…although I still think Stonebury is better suited as a family home.'

'Except that's not what we're in business for,' Tori pointed out.

'No.' Jasper sighed again, then glanced back over his shoulder as a burst of laughter cut through the air. Over the crest of the rolling hill behind them appeared a group of tourists, being led by Felix, presumably through to the Christmas market taking place around the old stable yard for the whole week before Christmas. The event was well signposted, but every year some visitors arrived at the wrong entrance and got promptly lost.

It was obviously Felix's turn to round them up and get them where they needed to be that afternoon.

Jasper grabbed her arm and led her further away, down to the edge of the river, as if he was afraid of being overheard. And remembering his behaviour in the kitchen, Tori realised he *was* afraid of just that.

What on earth was he about to tell her? What could make Viscount Darlton look *that* vulnerable?

The river was frozen, icy white and solid. A robin hopped across the frozen surface, searching for food. With the backdrop of the naked trees and the winter white sky, it looked for all the world like a scene from a Christmas card.

But Tori was too tense now to appreciate the beauty.

'What's going on?' she asked, when it became clear that Jasper wasn't about to talk without prompting.

He stopped beside a bench, looking out over the river to the woods beyond. Brushing a thin layer of powdery snow from the surface, he motioned for her to sit down, then sat beside her, close enough that his gloved hand lay beside hers.

'It's about my father,' he said slowly.

Tori rolled her eyes. 'I'd guessed that much. Is he ill? Is there anything I can do?'

'He's not…that's not what's going on.' Jasper took a deep breath, and swallowed so hard she saw his throat bob. Still staring out at the wintry scene ahead of them, he spoke so seriously, so deliberately that even Tori didn't dare interrupt.

'Five years ago I discovered that my father has another son, by a woman other than my mother. That son is Felix, and now the earl wants to make that knowledge public to the world.'

Tori blinked at him, and wished with all her heart that Henry had sent them off with a decent bottle of something highly alcoholic, too.

It looked as if they were going to need it.

Jasper wished he could say that telling Tori his family secret lightened the load he felt on his shoulders, but if anything hearing it out loud only made it feel more real. An inescapable hurricane about to rip his family and life apart because his father hadn't been able to keep it in his pants and had a misguided belief about the 'right thing' to do.

Tori stared at him. He stared back, waiting to see which way she was going to jump.

He realised, a little belatedly, that he was

putting an awful lot of trust in his beliefs about Tori Edwards. If she wasn't the sort of person he thought she was, then telling her even this much could bring about all the outcomes he'd come home to try and avoid.

He watched the emotions and thoughts flickering behind her eyes, and decided he was comfortable with the risk.

She wouldn't run to the papers. He was pretty much certain of that. Not only would it be detrimental to her own career—because he couldn't imagine the scandal was going to do a huge amount for Flaxstone Enterprises, either—but she wasn't that sort of person.

Exactly when he'd come to know Tori well enough to be sure of that…well, he could pinpoint it quite precisely, as it happened. It was last night, when she'd fallen apart in his arms, then put herself back together again.

'That's why you left,' she said finally. 'I always wondered.'

'I couldn't stay.' Jasper looked back out at the tiny robin, scratching the ice for food. 'I just… I didn't know how to deal with it. With any of it. My father, Felix, all the lies… I needed to be somewhere where I didn't care if people were lying or telling the truth. I needed to not care for a while.' Because he'd cared so damn much while he was at Flaxstone. All the conflicting emotions he'd experienced on finding out the truth had threatened to burn him up from the inside out, otherwise. 'Felix never told you?'

Tori shook her head. 'I had no idea. How did *you* find out?' He sensed it wasn't the question she *wanted* to ask, which only made him more nervous about what that would turn out to be. He had no doubt that she'd get around to it eventually.

'I came across a copy of my father's updated will on his desk one day. Talking about his two sons and heirs. The earl was away and I couldn't even talk to him about it until the next day.'

'That was the night you came to me,' Tori said, putting it together far quicker than he'd expected. 'I *knew* there was something different about you that night.'

Jasper looked down at his hands. 'I felt like a different person that night.'

'I liked the man I saw that night.' She pressed her gloved hand over his, and he gripped it tightly, grateful for the small show of comfort. 'So, the next day you confronted your father for a full confession?'

'Yeah. Of course. Why wouldn't I?'

Tori shrugged. 'Some people would prefer to pretend they'd never seen that paper, that they never knew the truth. Or save it for a later time when they could use the information.'

Jasper stared at her. He couldn't imagine doing anything other than seeking out the truth at that point. Secrets were bad enough. Why live with them longer than necessary or, worse, add another layer of deception to the whole situation? 'Would *you* have?'

'Probably not.' She gave him a wan smile. 'I just…sometimes the truth can be the worst thing to hear, you know?'

'I know,' he replied darkly. He remembered all too well that feeling, hoping against all the evidence that it would prove to be a mistake, that his father still had just the one child, only to find out that the truth was far worse than he'd even imagined.

His half-sibling wasn't some random stranger, conceived and born before his father had met his mother, or even through some awful affair since.

He was his best friend, the boy he'd grown up with. Felix.

'How did Felix take the news?' Tori asked, as if she'd read his mind. Or maybe his thoughts were just that clear on his face. He didn't hide things well—he knew that much about himself.

Unlike his half-brother.

'Turns out it wasn't quite the surprise for him that it had been for me.'

'He already knew?' Tori, at least, sounded suitably stunned at that revelation. 'When you asked if he'd told me, I assumed you meant *since* you left. But he knew before?'

Jasper nodded. 'I… I went to him first, of course.' It had been so natural. They'd been each other's confidant since they were small boys together. Felix had been there for him through every argument with his father, every incident at school, and Jasper had supported him too, against jibes from school mates about Felix being a scholarship boy—a scholarship funded, Jasper realised now, by their father—all the way to Felix's mother's death when they were seventeen, and the grief and torment that had followed. Felix knew all his secrets and he knew Felix's—or so he'd thought.

'I wanted to talk it all through with Felix before I approached my mother. I figured that he'd be as horrified as I was, that we could work through it together. But when I told him…there was no surprise behind his eyes. He turned pale, and, as I studied him, suddenly I could see all the signs I'd missed for so many years. He has our father's eyes, you know, if not his hair. And a certain look, sometimes, that's so like him…' Jasper shuddered.

'Anyway. I realised almost instantly that he already knew. I demanded to know when he found out, how long he'd been keeping it from me…that was the worst part, in lots of ways. The idea that my father and my best friend, two of the people who mattered most to me in the whole world, had been lying to me for so long. And I'd never even known…'

Tori let go of his hand and gripped the base of the bench, not looking at him as she asked, 'How long had he known?'

'Since his mother died. She knew how ill she was, couldn't leave him without ensuring he knew the truth. I guess she didn't trust my father to tell him, understandably.'

Felix had gone so completely off the rails after his mother's death. At the time, they'd all thought it was just the grief. But once Jasper had found out the truth, it all made so much more sense.

'So he knew for years before you did,' Tori said, thoughtfully. 'I can see how that would have hurt.'

Hurt seemed like such a small word for it. 'It was like I suddenly couldn't trust the whole world around me. Like my senses might be lying to me and up might actually be down. *Nothing* was the way I thought it was. I mean, I idolised my father, and I trusted Felix more than anyone, and suddenly neither of those things were true any longer.'

'What about your mother?'

Jasper stared down at his hands. 'I still don't know how much she actually knows. That's why I came back. Knowing Mum…even if she suspected something she'd pretend she didn't. You know what she's like.' Happy living in her own world, and stubborn enough to refuse to see anything beyond it. Even if hers was a world built entirely on lies and secrets. 'I suspect she'd prefer *not* to know the truth, to be honest.' That was how she'd always been. Jasper had learned young how to deal with her, and he'd stuck to those lessons even when his world had fallen apart.

'So you've never spoken to her about it?'

'No. But I'm going to have to. If my father publicly legitimises Felix the papers will grab that story and run with it—they always do. And then…'

'The whole world will know.' Tori pulled a face. 'Okay, I see why you came home. What I still don't get is why it meant you had to trash my meeting with your father.'

Okay, so one meeting probably wasn't the most important thing in the context of this conversation, but it was the piece of the puzzle Tori still didn't have, and she hated not knowing things that impacted her life and work.

If she'd realised exactly what was going on with Tyler sooner, maybe she'd have been able to stop it. Or maybe she wouldn't. But at least she'd have been working with all the facts. Instead, she'd assumed he was guilt-tripping her, when he'd told her he didn't know what he'd do without her. She'd never imagined that he'd actually meant that, without her there to keep him in check, he'd act out every stupid thing that passed through his head. And by the time she'd realised just how far he'd go, it was far too late.

Her heart ached for Jasper, so betrayed and alone. At the back of her mind she'd always wondered if him leaving had had anything to do with *her*, with that night they'd spent together. Now she knew he'd had far bigger worries than an ill-advised one-night stand. He wouldn't have been thinking about her at all.

Which, oddly, didn't make her feel as better as she'd imagined it would.

'Stonebury Hall,' Jasper said, with a sigh. 'I insisted on coming to look at it with you because I think it would be perfect for Mum. Somewhere she can ride out the media storm, get away from my father, and be safe.'

'All those battlements,' Tori mused. He wasn't wrong. Stonebury Hall was definitely a good place to hide out and take cover. But she couldn't help but think there was a better plan in there somewhere. If they worked together...

'Exactly. I want her safe.'

'But *she* wouldn't like it to look as if she was running and hiding.' Tori didn't know Lady Flaxstone very well, but from the comments she'd heard over the years she knew that her reputation was important to her. She wouldn't want people to think a scandal had driven her into hiding, even if it had.

'I know.' Jasper sounded frustrated. 'But if she's here, facing down the press at the door, or on the phone, the whole circus... We went through that once before, you know. When Father was involved in a business deal with an old friend that turned out to be *incredibly* ill-advised.' Tori knew the deal he meant. 'Ill-advised' might be the understatement of the century.

'How did your mother take it?'

'Badly,' Jasper said, flatly. 'Very badly. It didn't fit her perfect world view that she'd created, but she couldn't ignore it either, so she couldn't cope. She basically took to her bed for months, and that wasn't even personally connected to her, really. This? I'm worried it will break her.'

'So we get her out of here and up to Stonebury,' Tori agreed. 'But how about we give her a reason to be there, and a team to support her?'

Jasper frowned at her. 'How do you mean?'

The idea was coming together in her head now, so quickly Tori wondered how she hadn't seen it straight off. 'You're right that the main house at Stonebury is more like a home. So, you move in there with your mother to start with, get her set up with a trusted manager and assistants. Then when she's settled, you can head back to the States and your real life.' Tori pushed aside the tug on her heart as she mentioned him leaving. She almost wanted to offer to go, look after his mother herself, but she knew that the final decision on staffing, and particularly her assignments, would lie with the earl. 'But she's not just hiding out. The team are developing the barns and outbuildings—not to mention that fantastic old stable block—to provide spaces for craft workshops and stalls, a café, maybe a little farm shop. It can be named after your mother or something, give her a real connection to the place.'

Jasper stared at her in amazement. 'That

might…actually work. Why didn't I think of that?'

'Because you were scared, and too focussed on your immediate problem,' Tori replied promptly.

'I wouldn't say scared, exactly…' Jasper rolled his eyes. 'Fine. Maybe a little. Okay, so, we have a plan. How do we convince the earl?'

'We work up a killer proposal,' Tori said. 'Together.'

Suddenly, Jasper seemed very close, although neither of them had moved. Maybe it was the way his eyes seemed to grow warmer, as if he was looking deeper inside her. Or perhaps it was the soft smile that flickered around his lips. 'You think you can stand being stuck with me a little longer, then? While we work on the proposal, I mean.'

That wasn't all he meant. Tori could see the truth in his eyes.

He was thinking about last night. About that kiss.

And she had to admit, so was she.

God, I want to kiss him again.

'I think I could just about bear it,' she said, unable to tear her gaze away from his. Her mouth was dry, her throat too tight, and despite the snow and ice her face felt glowing warm.

'Who knows?' Jasper said, leaning in just a little closer. 'Maybe you'll even come to enjoy it.'

'I suppose miracles do happen,' Tori replied. Even if she'd never believed in miracles before. Suddenly this one felt inevitable.

CHAPTER NINE

'I CAN'T STARE at this thing any more.' Frustration oozed from Tori's very being.

Jasper put down the latest research he was reading—printed out, because if he had to stare at a screen for another moment his eyes might fall out—and studied her instead. It was a much more attractive prospect, anyway.

Her dark hair tumbled forward over her forehead, curling a little against her cheek, and her grumpy expression somehow served only to make her look more adorable. She looked tired—they were *both* tired—but beautiful, and suddenly Jasper knew that he couldn't waste another moment with her working. Not on such a gorgeous winter's day.

'Let's get out of here,' he said. She gave him a scandalised look. One thing he'd learned from working closely with Tori for the past few days was that she worked too damn hard, and too long. And he'd thought *he* was a workaholic. Apparently he had nothing on Tori.

'It's less than a week before Christmas,' he argued reasonably. 'And a *Saturday*. I think we're allowed a little time off for seasonal cheer.'

'You wanted to present this to your father before Christmas,' Tori pointed out.

'And we will. I mean, we're nearly there with this, right? All we're really doing now is double-checking the figures and making sure the research holds up.' Tori had been adamant that every I had to be dotted and every T crossed before they presented their ideas to the earl. There had to be no gaps, no wiggle room, if they wanted to pull this off.

Jasper totally agreed in principle. In practice, he needed fresh air, a break, and maybe even a cup of mulled wine.

'Come on,' he wheedled. 'We could head down to the Christmas market. It might even give us a stunning idea for that finishing touch you're still hankering for.'

Tori was adamant that there was still something missing from their proposal, something that would set it off perfectly and give them an unbeatable proposal the earl would have to go for.

Right now, Jasper would be happy with just

guilting his father into doing the right thing and giving his mother an out. But Tori insisted that it had to be good business sense, too.

Tori considered his suggestion, and Jasper could see in her expression the workaholic warring with the desire for a proper break.

'I'll buy you a mulled wine...' he tempted her, and she broke, tossing her papers down on the desk.

'Oh, fine. Come on, then. But I want a mince pie, too.'

'Have you spoken to your mother yet?' Tori asked as they strolled out through the hall's back door and down through the gardens to the market, out by what used to be farm outbuildings. Much of the Flaxstone land was still farmed by tenant farmers, but the structures they used these days were rather more efficient and well equipped than the more historic versions. Still, Tori and his father had found plenty of profitable ways to use the unneeded buildings, just as they had the rest of the estate.

'I've spoken to her about many things,' Jasper said evasively. 'Although she still won't tell me what she wants for Christmas. Apparently I should be able to surprise her.'

He knew that wasn't really what Tori was

asking, but for just ten minutes it would be nice to forget about his family's issues and enjoy her company. Something he'd found himself doing more and more over the last week, even while deep at work on the Stonebury project. He just liked being with her. Even if she wouldn't let them take their relationship any further. He wanted her there, with him.

He wasn't thinking too hard about what that meant.

'Jasper,' she said, a warning tone in her voice. 'You know what I mean. You *promised* me you'd talk to her about Stonebury before we put this proposal to your father, and you're running out of time. This isn't a decision you can make for her. You have to be sure that this is what she wants, too.'

'I know.' And he did. Tori was right—something that seemed to happen irritatingly often. 'I just…haven't found the right moment yet. I'll do it soon though. I promise.'

'And have you spoken to Felix?' Her tone was softer this time, and she slipped her arm through his as she asked. It was funny—but nice funny—the way that, as they'd grown closer as friends working together, they seemed to have become closer physically, too. These days, they always seemed to be finding reasons to touch each other—for comfort, for support, or just because they both seemed to need it.

Jasper could hardly imagine the closed-off woman he'd explored Stonebury with offering him a comforting touch. But that was before the Moorside. Before they shared their secrets.

Now, he wondered how far this casual contact would go. Would she kiss him again? Or let him kiss her?

The anticipation was so delicious he almost didn't want to rush it. Although other parts of him were rather more eager to progress...

He felt like a teenager again, or the much younger man who'd been lucky enough to experience Tori's touch the first time round. He remembered now that curiosity he'd felt towards her, the pull, the fascination he couldn't shake. The challenge she'd presented, with those stone walls up. The way the excitement he had felt building had eclipsed the realisation of his father's betrayal, that night she'd let him see behind her mask, just for a while...

Now, the mask was down. He'd discovered the real woman hiding behind the battlements—seen where she came from and discovered her secrets, her loss. And he liked her so much more for it.

A ridiculous amount more, really. Especially

considering he'd be leaving again in the new year, and she wouldn't even kiss him.

'Jasper?' Tori's concerned voice interrupted his consideration of all the other ways he might like her, and he started, jerking his gaze towards her. 'Felix? You spoke with him?'

'No. God, no.' He hadn't been able to look Felix in the eye before he'd left, and the two emails his ex-best friend had sent afterwards, presumably trying to explain himself, had been deleted unread. 'What is there to say?'

Tori gave him a long look. 'Maybe it's more about listening. Hearing his side of the story at last. Seeing if the two of you can find a way back to being friends again. I mean, I remember how close you used to be. Mrs Rawkins used to despair of the two of you. Even the night we...' She blushed, and Jasper found himself enchanted all over again. 'Well, when you came home with me, you had to text Felix to tell him where you'd be first.'

'That was mostly for bragging rights,' Jasper said absently. Then, off her eye roll, added, 'because I was an idiot. Obviously.'

'Oh, I never doubted that,' Tori replied. But there was a fondness to her tone that wouldn't have been there a couple of weeks ago, and it made him smile. 'Come on, speed up. It's cold and I want that mulled wine before we have to get back to work.'

She lengthened her stride and he matched it easily, keeping her hand tucked through his arm as they headed across the estate towards the festive strains of sleigh bells and carols.

It had been five long years since Jasper had visited the Flaxstone Christmas market, and it was clear that things had progressed a long way in his absence. When he'd left, the event had been a few small craft stalls, a poorly decorated tree, and the local junior-school choir singing Christmas carols. Now, the whole market wouldn't have looked out of place somewhere in one of Europe's capital cities. There was a small group of singers dressed in Victorian outfits performing under the oversized tree, which was strung with delicate, glowing white lights. A vintage-looking carousel took up one corner, with a queue of children and adults waiting to ride, and a full-on hog roast was on offer under one of the wooden shelters. The whole place was packed, and everyone Jasper saw was smiling—bar a small child who seemed to be scared of either Father Christmas, his real-life reindeer, or both.

A lot of that, he suspected, was to do with Tori. As they strolled through the Scandi-style wooden stalls, all stocking handmade decorations, gifts and edibles, many of the stallholders stopped to thank Tori for her assistance and support, and several handed over freebie treats in gratitude.

'Looks like you've been busy while I've been gone,' he observed, as another stallholder called them over and placed a paper bag in Tori's palm, with gushing thanks.

'There's still more I want to do.' She fished around in the bag and smiled at its contents. 'Ooh, apple and cranberry mince pies! These are so good. Anyway. Next year, I want to do a light display on the walk through the woods to get to the market, and maybe even look at siting the Santa's grotto in there too, with extra elves to help families find the way.'

'When have you had time to be working on the market?' Jasper asked as Tori handed him a pie from the bag. 'I mean, we've been working flat out on the proposal for days, and before that we were snowbound at the Moorside.'

Tori shrugged, wiping crumbs from around her mouth. 'Most of this was set up months ago. I always start working on Christmas in summer—and so do these guys. They need to know their plans so they can build stock, plan sales, schedule staff and so on. Christmas starts *long* before you think it does, you know. Sometimes I think it's actually an all-year event…' She trailed off, her eyes suddenly wide.

'What?' Jasper asked cautiously. That kind of look made him nervous.

'I've figured out what the proposal needs.' Tori beamed, and reached up to place her palms on either side of his face. Then, without any more warning, she stretched up on tiptoe and planted a firm kiss against his lips.

Jasper's body reacted with a jolt, and he forgot all about food and Christmas and Stonebury as he let himself luxuriate in the kiss. Then his brain caught up, and he wrapped his arms around her waist to hold her closer, and deepened their embrace.

Someone, somewhere, whooped appreciatively, and Tori pulled back, her cheeks bright pink. She stepped out of his arms, then grabbed his hand. 'Come on. We need to get back to work.'

We need to talk about that kiss. And do it again. Very soon.

But Jasper knew Tori. There'd be no discussion about what had just happened—or what could happen—between them until after she'd got this new idea down on paper.

After that, though, Jasper had plans.

* * *

'The proposal certainly looks interesting.' The earl put down the printout he'd been reading, lifted his glasses from his nose, and looked up at them. Tori forced her feet to stay planted on the centuries-old carpet. Shuffling from foot to foot wasn't good for her professional appearance *or* the flooring. 'And I must say I'm glad to see the two of you working together so well. That gives me hope for our future.'

He was looking at Jasper as he said it, Tori realised. Jasper, of course, was looking studiously out of the window over his father's left shoulder. It was pitch black outside, so she had no idea what he was even pretending to look at.

She muffled a sigh. She understood Jasper's anger and upset, of course she did. He had every right to be furious with his father for his actions, and maybe even angry with Felix for lying to him for so long. But she couldn't help but wish he was even a *little* willing to move beyond the events of the past and consider the future.

Of course, she wasn't sure if she'd have even had that thought if it hadn't been for two days at the Moorside Inn, revisiting her own past. And it wasn't as if she were rushing back there either, so who was she to judge? Sometimes the past was just too painful to live in—and too hard to leave behind. Jasper had run away, exactly the same as she had. He'd only come back to help his mother, and she'd only gone back to the Moorside because the snow had left her no other choice. Neither of them were exactly poster children for healthy forward momentum away from their issues. They just took their baggage with them when they ran.

And that would be fine. Except Liz and Henry were expecting her for Christmas now. And if Jasper couldn't move on from what his father had done…then he wouldn't be staying in the country much longer. He'd see his mother settled at Stonebury, if their plan worked. But beyond that? Tori had already made herself face up to the unwelcome truth that he'd be returning to his life in the States in the new year.

Another entry on a lengthy list of reasons why she mustn't let herself grow too attached to the Viscount Darlton. Right after the fact that 'Viscount' was his actual title. Not her world, not her people. She was staff, not family.

And she'd given up the only family she had left to achieve even that.

Plus there was his unfortunate habit of never

sticking with the same girl for more than a night or two, something that didn't seem to have changed while he'd been away, given that he was still single.

Not that she'd exactly been pursuing romance and true love since Tyler had died, either. Her one night with Jasper had been a one-off.

Except now she'd kissed him. Again. And that was definitely the sort of action that could lead to it being *more* than a one-off, if she let it.

Well. That was a very distracting line of thought. Tori forced herself to abandon it until later as the earl continued speaking.

'Which one of you came up with the idea for the Christmas tree farm?'

Tori snuck a look at Jasper, who returned it with a hint of a smile—the first she'd seen since they entered the office.

'It was very much a collaborative project, my lord,' she said, diplomatically. In truth, after that kiss she definitely wasn't thinking about, she'd dragged Jasper back from the Christmas market to the side sitting room they'd been using as their office and declared that they were going to create Christmas every day at Stonebury!

Jasper had looked at her as if she were crazy, until she'd explained.

'It's perfect for it. We set up a permanent Christmas village, smaller than the market here, but with crafts for sale and—this is the important part—workshops so people can make their own wreaths, decorations, gifts etc. in the months running up to Christmas. We could do other seasonal workshops too— Valentine's Day, Easter, that sort of thing. But the key would be Christmas, all year round. It's the novelty of it that will draw people in.'

Jasper had looked thoughtful. 'There was a small copse of fir trees behind the house, did you see? Apparently a previous owner had considered setting up a Christmas tree farm, but had to sell before it came to fruition. We could revive it, supplement it with bought-in trees until our own grew up enough...'

'And we could keep reindeer!' Tori had said excitedly.

Jasper had laughed and shaken his head. But Dasher, Dancer and their friends had made it into the proposal.

'Well, I like the work you've done, and the figures and research included. Obviously I imagine the farm shop and catering facilities would be subsidising the more...interesting parts of the project for a while. But if word gets around, it could become a novelty feature for tourists, one of those "must see if you're passing through" places. The location is good for that…'

'And there's a lot of local craftspeople always looking for new places to display and sell their wares. With more "buy local" initiatives springing up all the time, it would be good to be at the heart of that,' Jasper added, the first time he'd spoken directly to his father since the meeting had started.

'But you still want the house for…well, to be a personal dwelling, rather than part of the business?' the earl asked Jasper.

Tori bit her lip and waited to see how he'd answer. Would he even want his father to know that he'd told her everything?

'I want Mother to have somewhere to retreat to, that's all,' Jasper said. 'You owe her that much.'

If the earl was surprised at his candour in front of Tori, he didn't show it. Instead, he sighed, and said, 'Very well. Let me think it over. I'll let you know my decision in good time.'

Tori turned to leave, Jasper close behind her, his hand at the small of her back. It felt warm and protective—and absurdly sexy, given the smallness of the gesture.

'But, son?' the earl called suddenly, and she

felt Jasper stiffen behind her. 'I suggest you talk to your mother. While I'm considering.'

'Told you so,' Tori whispered as she was hurried out of the room.

'Yeah, yeah,' Jasper muttered back. 'Come on.'

'Where are we going now?'

'*We* are going for a drink. And *I* am going to celebrate by eating the last of Henry's pies.'

'So you're not going to *share* the pie?' Tori's voice was plaintive as she stared at his loaded plate across the kitchen table.

'Nope.' Jasper gave her a gleeful smile, and tucked in.

Mrs Rawkins had rolled her eyes when the two of them had bowled in and Tori had raided the wine cellar, while he'd retrieved the pie he'd dug out of the freezer earlier to defrost. She'd declared she was done for the night so, as long as they cleared up after themselves, she didn't care what they got up to.

'But my kitchen better be exactly as I left it,' she'd warned as she'd put on her coat. 'I've got staff coming in from everywhere to prepare for the party tomorrow night—and don't you touch *any* of the food we've got prepped in the fridges. Okay?' Tori and Jasper had nodded, mutely. Jasper had felt about sixteen again as she'd given them one last glare before sweeping out.

Mrs Rawkins needn't have worried. Jasper's priorities for the evening were quite simple. Eat this pie—while making Tori watch. Share a bottle of wine with a beautiful woman. And hopefully get her to talk about and maybe repeat that kiss.

After that, all he wanted to do was fall into bed—even if he was alone. Although he wouldn't say no to company if Tori offered... The last few days of extreme work hours were catching up with him, and Mrs Rawkins wasn't the only one who needed to prepare for tomorrow night's party. As the heir to the Flaxstone estate, he knew there'd be expectations placed on him—even if he'd successfully avoided them for the past five years.

And he needed to talk to his mother. Tori was right; he couldn't put that off any longer.

'A decent man would at least let me try a bite,' Tori tried again.

'A decent woman wouldn't have stolen fifty per cent of my pies,' Jasper pointed out, between mouthfuls. 'Although I guess I could always go back to the Moorside and ask Henry for more...'

The teasing look disappeared from Tori's face at that, and she reached for the bottle of red wine they'd opened and topped up both their glasses.

'Or you could bring me some when you go back for Christmas,' he pushed.

'What's the point?' Tori asked. 'You'll be heading back to the States as soon as your mother is settled at Stonebury, assuming the earl agrees to our plan.'

'I'd come back for this pie,' Jasper said appreciatively, taking another mouthful. Then he caught sight of Tori's expression. 'Unless you don't want me to leave?'

They hadn't talked about this. Hadn't talked about the future. Hadn't even talked about them as a thing that was edging ever closer to happening. Jasper was almost certain she felt it as much as he did, but, apart from that excited kiss at the Christmas market, there'd been no sign that Tori was willing to move any further, and so Jasper had waited.

Until now.

'You need to live your life wherever makes you happiest,' she said, with a shrug. She didn't meet his gaze though. 'And I can't see that being here once your father makes his big announcement about Felix.'

'Well, no, probably not,' Jasper admitted.

Maybe he was wrong about the wider public's appetite for aristocratic scandal, but he doubted it. And even if he was, *local* society would definitely care. That was the society Lady Flaxstone cared about most.

He'd take his mother away with him to the States if he could, but her fear of flying verged on the phobic, and she'd be miserable away from her own country. He hadn't really thought beyond getting her settled at Stonebury, but if Tori took on the project personally, he could definitely see himself visiting regularly…

'So I only have to put up with you and your cruel pie eating for another few weeks, I figure,' she said, staring longingly at his pie.

Rolling his eyes, Jasper loaded up the fork again and held it out across the table to her.

'Really?' she asked, eyes suddenly bright. From the excitement on her face a person couldn't have been blamed for thinking he'd just offered her the crown jewels, or a sparkly engagement ring.

'Go on,' he said indulgently.

Tori's eyes fluttered closed as she wrapped her mouth around the fork. 'So, so good,' she muttered as she chewed.

Jasper had to agree. If it meant he could see that look of bliss on her face every day, he'd start shipping in Henry's pies by the dozen.

Or maybe he'd just concentrate on finding some other things he could do for her that made her look that way…

Tori swallowed, opened her eyes and smiled at him. 'Thank you. I know how hard it is for you to share.'

'Is that another not so subtle hint that I should talk to my mother and/or half-brother?' Tori hadn't exactly been restrained on the subject until now. Despite her comment, he trusted that she knew him well enough that the issue of going from only child to youngest son wasn't the problem here. According to the will he'd found, his father intended to split the inheritance fairly equally between them, with Flaxstone going to Jasper, and as the only *legitimate* son the title was his by law anyway, whatever his father did.

'Yes,' Tori admitted. 'But not tonight.'

That surprised him. 'No? How did I earn this reprieve? By giving you pie?'

'Basically.' She gave him an impish grin. One that reminded him of the first night they'd ever spent together—before all the secrets that had torn his life apart. 'But mostly, I want you to finish this bottle of wine with me.'

Something in her smile gave him hope. 'And then?'

'Then…maybe you'll walk me home?'

'I can do that. It's only gentlemanly, after

all.' Then he reached behind him, grabbed another knife and fork from the drawer, and handed them over. Pushing his plate to the centre of the table, he waited for Tori to help herself to his pie before taking his own mouthful.

Maybe he could get good at sharing after all.

CHAPTER TEN

FLAXSTONE HALL WAS silent as they let themselves out of the back door, and followed the darkened path towards Tori's gatehouse cottage. Tori wasn't sure if it was the wine or the sneaking around that made her want to giggle so badly. But she and Jasper were both grown adults, and it wasn't as if they hadn't done this before, anyway.

Memories of the last time they'd snuck down to her cottage only made her feel warmer despite the chill of the night.

God, what was she doing? Was she really going to invite Jasper in for a nightcap—and more?

Well, yes. Yes, she was.

Because he might be leaving soon, but that was probably a good thing. The Jasper she'd got to know over the last week or two was far too tempting, too risky. Given long enough she knew she could fall for him—and fall hard.

It was, she could admit now—to herself, anyway—exactly what she'd been afraid of five years ago. He was so gorgeous, so charming, and had a way of making her feel as if she were the only person in the world when he flirted with her. If she'd let her defences down for a second she could have found herself in love with him, and ripe for having her heart broken like all the others girls he'd paraded through Flaxstone.

That was why she'd run away, after their night together. She'd had to protect her heart. And if he'd woken up, sober, in her bed and still wanted her, still smiled at her the same way he had the night before, she'd have been a goner. And if he hadn't…well, Tori wasn't entirely sure that wouldn't have been worse.

But now, now she was older, wiser, and she knew this thing had a time limit. She could risk one more night with Jasper, as long as her head and her heart both understood that was all it could be.

Because even if he stayed, she wasn't looking for love, not again. And she *definitely* wasn't looking for a long-distance relationship. She'd tried that with Tyler and—she wasn't thinking about Tyler tonight.

She wasn't thinking about the past *or* the future tonight.

She was thinking about right now, and how good Jasper's arm felt around her waist as they stumbled down the path, and how much she wanted to kiss him again.

Stay in the moment, Tori.

The security light Felix had helped her install, after a fox started getting into her bins, flared to life as they crossed the threshold into its sensors. Jasper jumped, making Tori laugh, until he wrapped her up in his arms and suddenly she didn't have the breath for laughter.

'So, I've walked you home,' he said, his forehead resting against hers as he looked down into her eyes. 'This is the part where you have to decide if you want to invite me in or not.'

And even though she'd already made that decision, the moment she'd asked him to walk down to her cottage with her, Tori hesitated.

'Do you *want* to come in?' she asked.

'More than anything.' She could hear the sincerity in his voice. 'God, Tori, you have to know I've been thinking of practically nothing but kissing you again ever since—' He broke off.

'The other day at the Christmas market?' she guessed, but Jasper shook his head.

'Since you kissed me at the Moorside,' he admitted. 'Even though I knew that wasn't about me, that it didn't mean what I hoped it might mean, I couldn't stop thinking about how incredible it felt to have you in my arms. And imagining all the things I'd do if I got the opportunity again, when the timing was better.'

He'd been thinking about her since then? Even when they'd been clashing in his father's study, or when she'd been working for too many hours straight on the proposal and had rubbed her eyes until her mascara had smudged into black rings around her lashes and she hadn't noticed until she'd got home?

He'd been thinking about her. The same way she'd been thinking about him.

Imagining him.

'The timing seems pretty much perfect right now,' she said, the words coming out breathier than she'd intended.

'That's exactly what I thought.'

He met her gaze head-on as he lowered his lips to hers, obviously watching for a sign that she wanted him to stop, or take things slower. But she didn't, so she raised herself up on her tiptoes to meet him halfway, falling into a kiss that seemed to have been years in the making.

It hadn't been like this the last time they were here, Tori realised. She hadn't known him then the way she did now—hell, he wasn't even the same person, really. Too much had happened in the last five years.

But in a way, she was glad he'd left, after that one night they'd spent together.

Because it meant they could be the people they were now, and they could have this perfect, mind-blowing kiss.

After long, long, blissful moments, Jasper pulled back, putting just enough distance between them to whisper. 'So. Are you going to invite me in?'

Tori smirked. 'Invite? I think I'm going to have to insist on it.'

Jasper grinned back at her, his eyes bright and alive like she remembered from before he'd left Flaxstone.

'Works for me,' he said.

This time, when Jasper woke up in Tori's bed in her cosy gatehouse cottage, she was still beside him, gloriously naked and tangled in sheets and blankets and his arms.

Just another reason why this time had been so much better than the last. Add in five years of maturity, experience—and a far deeper understanding of each other—and the night had been, well, glorious. So much more than he'd expected, even yesterday.

'You okay?' Tori mumbled, turning over

and looking blearily up at him. 'I mean, was everything…okay?'

'More than.' He pressed a kiss against her bare shoulder, then moved his lips up towards her ear. 'Better than the best steak and ale pie in the country,' he whispered, and she laughed.

God, he loved that sound. Loved seeing her, hearing her, free from secrets and the past and inhibitions. They'd told each other everything now. She knew about Felix and his dad, and he knew about the boyfriend who died, who'd made her close herself off to the world.

He'd looked behind the battlements and discovered the real Tori Edwards. And he didn't think he'd ever stop being grateful that she'd let him.

'Do you think you can get me some more of those pies, though, when you go back for Christmas Day?' he asked.

She rolled her eyes. 'If I go. And if you're still here when I get back.'

'You might not go?' Jasper frowned. He'd thought she'd made her peace with Liz and Henry, found some closure. He didn't like the idea of her being all alone in the world again once he returned to the States. Not when that meant the only family she had was his dysfunctional one.

Tori sighed. 'I'm not sure it would be a good

idea. And besides, they gave me my Christmas present already, remember? Wrapped and packed in the car when I wasn't supposed to be looking.'

'You don't think they're expecting you to show up either,' Jasper said, piecing it together. 'But why not? Because of Tyler?'

At that, Tori tumbled out of bed, keeping one of the blankets tucked around her, and flashed him a quick smile. 'Let's not worry about this now. We have the party to look forward to tonight. I need to survive that before I can even *think* about Christmas Day.'

She was deflecting, he realised. Leading him away from the question.

Suddenly he wondered if she *had* told him everything about why she'd left the Moorside, after all. And if she would even tell him if he asked.

More secrets. Great.

The happy, relaxed and sated feeling he'd woken up with started to ebb away, leaving him tense and awkward again. He sat up, as Tori gathered his clothes together from where they'd been scattered on the floor, and handed them to him.

'You can use the shower first, if you like,' she said, with a false brightness. 'After all, you need to go talk to your mother this morning. But I'll see you tonight for the party.'

Then she disappeared towards the kitchen, and he heard the kettle flick on.

Brilliant.

Jasper swung his legs over the side of the bed. Given how quickly his perfect morning had deteriorated, he supposed he'd better go have that conversation with his mother before things got any worse.

Tori heard the cottage's front door close quietly behind Jasper, and let out a sigh of relief. Then, she tipped the coffee she'd made him down the sink, and took her own cup to the tiny kitchen table where she could look out of the window at Flaxstone in the snow and think. Something she'd apparently been doing too little of lately.

The euphoria and hope of the night before had worn off quickly in the early morning light. It had felt so right, so easy, waking up beside him. The peace of a snowy winter's day outside her window, and the warmth of his arms around her. Like the Moorside again, only better.

As if it was where they were meant to be.

What *had* she been thinking, bringing Jasper back here last night? Well, she knew the answer to that. She'd been thinking that he was gorgeous, she was insanely attracted to him, still, and she wanted him in her bed again. And she'd *also* been thinking that he was leaving soon. That he'd disappear back to the States and leave her and her mess of a history behind without another thought.

Because the truth was, as much as she hated the thought of Flaxstone without him again, it would probably be the best thing for both of them.

He was too invested, too deep into her personal life already. Tori had always kept that side of her—Vicky's side, as she thought of it—walled off, for a very good reason. Because of the pain of the memories, of course, and because of the guilt. Because of the way Jasper—or anyone—would look at her if they knew how she was responsible for Tyler's death. But mostly because she knew it could all too easily happen again.

She *wanted* things. She wanted success, she wanted a career, she wanted to go places and see things and do stuff that her mother could only have dreamed of. Even if, so far, she hadn't quite made it out of Yorkshire. It was that selfishness that had killed Tyler.

And it hadn't changed.

She'd tried—really she had. Straight after

his death, she'd vowed she'd never put her personal ambition above what her loved ones wanted again. But that wasn't who she was. She was Victoria Edwards and she *wanted*. No amount of love could change that, and eight years definitely hadn't.

Which was why it wasn't fair to get involved with people, not when she knew that she'd always choose her own ambition over them, and only end up getting them hurt. Or dead, in Tyler's case.

He'd told her, to her face, that if she left for university bad things would happen. That he wouldn't cope without her. And he'd been right.

But she'd gone anyway.

A better life for her meant a worse life for other people. But she was such a terrible person that she *still* couldn't stop wanting.

She'd wanted Jasper. But this morning, hearing him ask about Henry and Liz and Christmas at the Moorside, she'd realised what a mistake that was.

Jasper couldn't be an anonymous one-night stand. Even last time he'd been a risk, but she'd wanted so badly she'd taken it anyway, and lucked out when he'd left without seeing her again. He'd always been too desperate to break through her walls—through curiosity more than anything, she suspected. Jasper hated anyone having secrets he didn't know and understand—just look at his reaction to the news about Felix.

What would he do if she told him hers? Explained exactly why this couldn't happen again?

Tori had a horrible feeling she was going to find out, and soon. Certainly before he left for America again. Because Jasper never let secrets stay hidden.

Jasper found his mother exactly where he expected to find her: settled on the loveseat in her small sitting room, looking out over the gardens, a tea tray at her side and a murder mystery novel in her hands. Mornings were sacred to Lady Flaxstone. In the afternoons, she'd busy about with local events, estate business, fundraising, visits and so on. But the mornings were entirely hers and not to be disturbed.

'I'm not a morning person,' he remembered her saying once, when he'd asked her about it. 'I don't even like my own company in the mornings. Why would I enjoy anyone else's?'

Perhaps, with hindsight, he should have waited until this afternoon to broach the subject of Felix's legitimisation with her, but now he was here, all he wanted to do was get it over with.

'Mother?'

Lady Flaxstone looked up, obviously surprised at being interrupted. 'Jasper? What's happened? Is something the matter?'

He forced a smile onto his face, and took the small armchair opposite her. He always felt as if this sitting room had been designed for a race of humans about three quarters the size of the average. He was a giant in this space.

Or maybe his mother had just wanted to make it uncomfortable for other people, so she wouldn't be disturbed. He wouldn't put it past her. She always did create her own world, her own reality, exactly the way she wanted to believe it could be.

'I wanted to talk to you about Father,' he said, not entirely sure where to start. 'And... and Felix.'

'Ah.' His mother put down her book and gave him her full attention. 'I was rather wondering when you would. You've been back three weeks now, after all. But I suppose you've been rather preoccupied with our Tori, haven't you?'

Jasper blinked. Perhaps his mother's shaping of reality didn't mean she was *completely* oblivious to the real world after all. He frowned, as the thought tickled another at the back of his brain. One he couldn't quite put his finger on, just yet.

'Dad has spoken to you about it, then, I assume? What he plans to do? And about, well, Felix's parentage.' He'd always assumed that his father would have been forced to tell her *something* about why he'd left home so abruptly. He'd hoped it would be the truth, although he had no idea how his mother would take the news.

'Of course.' His mother sounded surprised he even had to ask. 'We discussed it at length before he emailed to tell you. I wanted to ensure that your inheritance was still secure— of Flaxstone, and the title. As much as I love Felix, and agree it's only fair he gets a decent share of the rest of the money and land, Flaxstone really *is* yours by rights.' She gave him a sideways look. 'Although I rather think your father feels that Felix has done more for it over the last five years, and not without reason.'

A strange cold feeling ran through Jasper's veins. 'You…agree with Father?'

'Of course. You didn't think he'd have decided to do this without consulting me, did you?' Her eyes widened as she took in his expression. 'Oh, you did.'

'You know what Father's like,' Jasper replied, thinking his way through the thought process that had led him here. 'He just decides a thing and goes for it. No consultation, no consideration of others.'

'That's how he *used* to be,' Lady Flaxstone agreed. 'But, Jasper, you have to understand that your leaving changed him. Maybe not as much as you'd like, but it *did* change him. And me, for that matter. Have you really not noticed since your return?'

'No.'

Because I've been avoiding him as much as possible, just as Tori said.

Lady Flaxstone's expression turned harder. 'You leaving us… I'm not saying I don't understand why you felt you needed to get away, but I *do* wish you'd at least talked to us—to me, or even to Felix—before you went.'

'I—I didn't want to drag you into the whole sordid mess. I knew Father would have to tell you everything once I'd gone, but I hoped that he'd find a way to keep you protected from the worst of it. Which was why I was so furious when he emailed with his plans to tell the world.'

'Jasper…' His mother sighed. 'Flaxstone has been my whole world, ever since I came here as a bride. Do you honestly believe I wouldn't be aware and alert to everything that happens under its roof?'

'I…no.' And there it was. That niggling thought slotted right into place and something stabbed Jasper around chest level. 'Wait. Are you saying you *always* knew about Felix?'

'Probably before your father did. Anna, Felix's mother, and I were always close, and I have four younger siblings—I knew the signs of a pregnancy better than most, even if I hadn't been going through it myself by then.'

'You knew.' She'd known who Felix was his whole life and had never told *either* of them. *So many secrets…* 'Did Father know that you knew?'

'Not at first. When he first brought me here as his bride…it wasn't entirely a love match, you realise. Oh, we liked each other well enough, and I had faith that we could *grow* to love one another, but beyond that… It was the fact that I had money, you see, and Flaxstone categorically didn't.'

He'd known all this, Jasper realised, somewhere at the back of his mind, somewhere he'd never examined it properly. Because from the earliest time he could remember, his parents had been a team, his father doting, his mother supportive. It felt too strange to imagine a time before that.

'But when Anna started to show I sat him down, told him I knew the baby had to be his. There had been plenty of hints, you see—whispered conversations I wasn't meant to hear, Anna's tears and her refusal to talk to me about it. I knew. And when he realised that…he crumpled. He really did care for her, you know, but not more than he cared for Flaxstone.'

'But he let them stay? Knowing that *you* knew that she was his mistress and Felix his child?'

'*I* let them stay,' Lady Flaxstone corrected him. 'In fact, I insisted on it.'

'Why?' he asked. But even as he said the word, he realised he already knew. She'd shaped reality to fit how she believed the world of Flaxstone ought to be. He'd thought she'd been avoiding the real world. In fact, she'd been working it like a blacksmith with a hammer, beating it into the weapon she needed to defend her version of reality.

'The relationship was over the day we got married, and I never saw a hint that it started up again afterwards. Anna even married, briefly, although it didn't work out. I didn't see why she should be punished for something your father was equally responsible for. And Felix *is* his son, whether he's publicly acknowledged or not. How could I ask your father to cast him out to the world and never see him again? And once you and Felix grew to be so close… I was sure I'd made the right decision. Until you left.'

For the first time in the conversation, his mother looked uncertain—and Jasper had no way to reassure her. Had she made the right choice? He couldn't know.

But one thing he did know for sure: everyone else had known the truth about his family except him. Everyone he cared about had been lying to him, in some cases for his entire life.

And he wasn't sure if he could ever forgive them for that.

'You should have told me,' he said numbly, stumbling to his feet as he headed for the door. 'You should have told me.'

CHAPTER ELEVEN

TORI BUSIED HERSELF with her usual work around the estate that day. It might be three days before Christmas, but in lots of ways that just meant there was more work to be done. The Christmas market would be packing down that afternoon, and the ballroom was being set up for the traditional Flaxstone Christmas party that evening. Yes, the estate staff and contractors had everything perfectly under control, but that didn't mean she shouldn't check in on them all once or twice. Or every half hour.

Eventually, she'd annoyed everyone enough that she needed to find something new to do, so she joined Mrs Rawkins' team in the kitchens, where she was relegated to assembling some of the easier canapés on lemongrass skewers. And that was where the earl found her.

'Oh, I adore these ones!' He cheerfully popped a canapé into his mouth, then grabbed a spare napkin and filled it with a few more. 'For later,' he explained with a wink.

'Can I help you, Your Lordship?' Mrs Rawkins's words were scrupulously polite, but her expression and tone made her disapproval perfectly clear. Tori hid a smile behind a napkin.

'Actually, I just wanted to borrow Tori, if you can spare her.'

Mrs Rawkins brightened. 'By all means!' she said, leading Tori to conclude she hadn't been as much help as she'd thought here, either.

She followed the earl back up to his office. He munched his way through his pilfered canapés as they walked, making it impossible for her to start a conversation. Once they were seated on either side of the desk, the door closed, however, the earl didn't beat around the bush.

'I've considered your proposal, and there's much to approve of in it, as always.'

'Thank you, Your Lordship.' A niggling feeling of guilt made her add, 'But if we're going to talk about the Stonebury proposal, Jasper really should be here too.'

'I'll talk to Jasper separately. Later.' The earl looked uncomfortable. 'I believe he spoke to his mother this morning and then took himself off for a walk. We assume he'll be returning this time, but…' He shrugged, and the niggle in her stomach only grew worse.

Of course he was coming back. Wasn't he?

'I think there's a lot of merit in the Christmas craft farm, and I even agree that the main house might be best kept as a personal dwelling. And Lady Flaxstone has expressed some interest lately in getting more involved with wider estate projects, so this might well win her approval. And if she wants to go and stay at the hall for a while, for whatever reason, I won't stop her. But Lady Flaxstone does not have the necessary business knowhow to get the place up and running and making a profit, even with a good manager there. In fact, it's clear to me that if this new venture is to be a success, it must have a talented, enthusiastic and dedicated leader on site to run it.' He leant over the desk a little towards her, before adding in a whisper, 'That's you, by the way.'

Tori blinked. 'Me?'

'Yes, you, Tori Edwards. As much as I'd like to keep you here making my life run smoothly for the rest of my years, you're far too talented for that. It's time for you to spread your wings and start running your *own* business ventures—or at least running one of mine for me to start with. Later, we'll see what sort of deal can be done, if you want it. Otherwise it will be good experience—and lucrative enough, I hope—for you to take flight and set up on your own, if you decide to.'

Her own business. Control and autonomy and the ability to really make a success of something she believed in. Wasn't this why she had left the Moorside Inn in the first place? She'd worked hard for the earl, and it was paying off with everything she'd ever dreamed of.

'I do have one or two conditions, however,' he added, and the hope that had sprung into her heart started to fade, just a little.

'Of course. And they are?'

'I want you to take Felix with you. You'll need a right-hand man and he's worked hard at learning the farming side of the business.'

'And that's the one part of it I haven't got much experience in.' Practically and businesswise, it made sense. Except for one thing. 'But if the point of the exercise is to get Lady Flaxstone away from any potential scandal—' She broke off as the earl raised his eyebrows.

They'd never actually said that in the proposal. They'd hinted at it, sure, and Jasper had implied it in his tone and expression, but they'd never said it. Jasper had never even confirmed that he'd told Tori the whole sordid story.

'I think my son will find that his mother is

stronger than he thinks. My *other* son, however…' He sighed. 'Felix has never had to experience that kind of media scrutiny before. And I'm fairly sure he has no desire to now. For his sake, I'd like him somewhere less…obvious for a while. Besides which, I want him to get to know all the corners of our estate business. After all, if Jasper refuses to come home for good…' He shrugged, but he'd said enough.

The earl was grooming Felix to take Jasper's place if Jasper refused it.

And he wanted her to help. He was offering her the best opportunity of her professional career and, oh, but she wanted it.

But she knew Jasper would never forgive her if she took it. For taking his father's side over his. Choosing Felix's well-being over Jasper's. For ruining the plan they'd worked so hard to develop together.

And as evidenced, Jasper wasn't the forgiving kind.

But then, Jasper wouldn't be here much longer. Would he?

'I need…may I take a little time to think about it?'

The earl gave her an amused look and she suspected that he somehow knew exactly what the situation was between her and Jasper. Knew exactly what he was asking her to do.

Damn him.

'Of course,' he said. 'Enjoy the party tonight, but let me know your decision before you leave—for the Moorside, I understand? We can call it my Christmas present.'

The whole downstairs of Flaxstone Hall was a hive of activity. Jasper weaved his way through caterers, waiting staff, event planners moving decorated trees taller than him, and a few family members who'd arrived early and would stay for the duration.

He needed to find Tori.

She'd been weirdly absent all afternoon—finally Mrs Rawkins had told him that the earl had dragged her off to his office, but after that it seemed no one had seen her at all. She hadn't been at her cottage when he'd knocked, either.

But she *must* be back there by now, surely, if she had any hope of being ready for the party on time.

Jasper was already dressed in his dinner jacket and bow tie, ready for the festivities. And for a drink, actually. But first, Tori.

'Jasper?' The voice caught him just as he was about to exit the front door, and it made him wince. He turned slowly, to face the half-brother he'd been pretending didn't exist for five long years, even since his return.

'Felix.'

His search for Tori—including a long ramble through the woods in case she'd gone for a walk—had given him plenty of time to think. About Tori, about his parents—and about Felix.

He'd thought about Tori, and how she'd stayed away from the Moorside, from her family, for so long after Tyler's death, because it hurt too much to be there. Was that why *he'd* stayed away? He'd concluded it was only part of it.

Mostly, he'd stayed away because he'd been too angry not to.

But after his conversation with his mother that morning, some of that anger had started to ebb away. Not all of it, not by a long way. And he still wanted to protect his mother, and the family reputation, from any media fallout after his father's announcement.

The only real thing that had changed was that he knew now he couldn't go on blaming Felix for something that had happened before his birth, or for not sharing a secret he knew could blow up their whole lives.

What would I have done in his place?

That was the question that had made him think the most. Would he have done things differently in Felix's place? In fact, in Felix's place, discovering his whole life had been a lie, would he have thought about how his friend was affected at all? Probably not.

Maybe the real problem was that he didn't know where to direct his anger, now he knew the real story behind it all.

'Mrs Rawkins said you were looking for Tori?' Felix asked, eyeing Jasper cautiously, as if waiting for him to explode. Jasper couldn't entirely blame him.

He really needed to talk to Felix. Maybe see if there was anything left of their friendship they could salvage.

But after he'd talked to Tori.

'Yes. Have you seen her?'

'Your mother gave her a room in the main house for the night, to get ready for the party. She's up in the Yellow Room, if you want her.'

Felix turned to go away, and Jasper found himself suddenly eager to make him stay.

'Thank you,' he called belatedly.

Felix looked back, a bemused smile on his face. 'You're welcome.'

Civility. That was a start, right? It was something.

And now he needed to talk to Tori.

He needed to know why she'd closed herself off to him again that morning. Whether she honestly expected him to just leave again like last time, as if their time together had never happened.

Because he couldn't.

Not now, not when he knew her. Not when he'd finally got her to lower those walls the whole way and let him in. Not when he knew, at last, how spectacular the woman waiting behind them was.

Because he'd realised something else out on his walk.

Flaxstone was where he belonged. And maybe, just maybe, Tori might belong there with him.

He just had to find a way to tell her that, to convince her of it, without her throwing those defensive walls back up again.

Tori reached behind her to tug up the zip of her evening dress, and failed to get it past about halfway. Wriggling the dress up a little, she stretched further, until her shoulder popped, trying to see the tiny silver zipper in the mirror, her head twisted almost all the way around.

Still no dice.

Sighing, she allowed her body to return to its more normal position and concluded that this was simply not a dress for one person. She'd have to sneak down to the kitchens with a wrap over her and find someone there to help her with it, once she'd finished perfecting her hair and make-up.

Or not. A knock at the door let her reconsider, and when she opened it a crack to see Jasper on the other side, looking handsome and irresistible in his dinner jacket, her heart thumped against her chest.

This was perfect. He could help her do up her dress—or undo it first, if he liked. There was still time, right? As long as she kept protecting her heart, made it clear this was just a festive fling, just sex and nothing more, what harm could one more night do?

But even as she smiled at him and opened the door, another part of her brain was already arguing back.

I can't lead him on. I can't let him think there's something between us—even if it is just sex—not without telling him about his father's offer. Not without admitting I'm thinking about taking it.

'You look beautiful,' he said, his gaze scanning her dress, her heels, her dark hair pinned back from her face before falling around her shoulders. He'd never seen her so dressed up, she realised.

'You scrub up reasonably well too, I suppose,' she replied, with a smirk. She needed to keep things light, familiar. He was already looking a little wary—not that she could blame him after the way she'd hurried him out of her cottage, and her bed, that morning.

Tori knew she was being unfair, inconsistent, not letting him know where he stood. And she hated it, probably as much as he did. But she didn't *know* where either of them stood.

Or where they'd be if she took the job his father had just offered her.

Would he leave without another word, as he'd done last time? Or would he argue with her, the way Tyler had when she'd made the decision to leave the Moorside, trying to wear her down with threats and promises and accusations?

She couldn't think about it now.

Focus on tonight. Focus on the party. Worry about tomorrow tomorrow. It'll be here soon enough.

'I could do with your help, actually.' She turned her bare back towards him, motioning towards the zip, but he made no move to fasten it.

In fact, his hands slipped between the material and her skin, skimming up over her ribs and cupping her breasts as he bent in to kiss her neck.

Tori leaned into his touch, the tingles he was

sending through her body happily distracting her from the moral dilemma buzzing around her head.

She needed to make a decision soon, she knew that. But maybe not *right* now. Maybe she could have this with Jasper just once more, just one more perfect night in his arms, before she had to ruin it all.

Tori turned and kissed him, and let him blot out all her thoughts for a while.

Whatever weirdness had been between him and Tori that morning faded away the moment Jasper touched her. Whatever she'd been hiding from, she wasn't running any more.

At least, until afterwards.

'A guy could get a complex, you know,' he said, as she slipped out of bed and pulled that damn dress back on. 'The way you're always so keen to get *out* of bed with me, I mean.'

The smile she flashed him didn't quite reach her eyes. 'We don't want to be late for the party.'

That's not why you're running.

Trouble was, he didn't know the real why. What was Tori hiding now? Too many secrets, all over again. And just when he thought he might have uncovered the last of his family's secrets.

'I suppose you're right.' Jasper sat up, lounging against the bedhead for a moment to watch her dress. If she wanted to pretend that everything was fine, he could do that. But he knew it wasn't just her clothes that were going back on.

Her mask was in place too. Her defences, her armour.

She was hiding again. Even this morning, she hadn't pulled the drawbridge up so completely.

So what's changed since then?

'I haven't seen you all day,' he observed as she shimmied the dress over her hips. He forced himself not to get too distracted by the motion, or the bare skin on display, but he couldn't stop himself looking. 'What have you been up to?'

Tori shrugged her bare shoulders. 'You know. Work. Lots to do for the party tonight.'

Except she hadn't been anywhere around the hall when he was looking for her, and, as far as he knew, the party had been almost entirely organised by his mother's event planner, same as every other year.

Tori backed up to the bed, that same zip dangling. This time, he did it up. Putting temptation out of reach, and completing her retreat into her armour all over again.

'What about you?' she asked, crossing again to the dressing table. He watched her reflection in the mirror as she threaded long silver earrings through her lobes.

Like chain mail.

Was everything about this woman armour? 'Did you talk to your mother?'

The question jerked him out of his reverie. 'I did, actually.'

'And?'

And she's been lying to me my whole life. Just like you're lying to me right now.

'And it turns out there was more to the story than I realised. She knew all along that Felix was the earl's son.'

Tori spun round to face him, her eyebrows high. '*Really?* And she still let them stay?'

'It was her idea, apparently.' Jasper swung his legs off the bed and reached for his trousers. 'She forgave him the affair, and didn't want Felix to suffer.'

'Huh.'

Jasper looked up to see her brow creased in a frown. 'What?'

'She forgave him. Like, properly. I didn't see that coming.'

'What were you expecting?' Jasper tilted his head to the side to watch her as she considered her answer. Maybe her mask wasn't quite as complete as it usually was—or perhaps he'd simply learned to see through it, somewhat—

because her thoughts were almost telegraphed across her expression. Confusion, doubt, and something Jasper couldn't quite put his finger on. Something that might even have been... hope?

'I don't know. Maybe that kind of grudging forgiveness where people say they understand because it's too late to say anything else. I mean, what difference could it make now, being angry, when the misdeed is almost thirty years in the past and nothing can change it? But she forgave him *then*, right when it happened. I... I just didn't expect that.'

'Neither did I,' Jasper admitted.

What did it say about them that neither had considered that sort of unconditional forgiveness as even a possibility?

'So...does she not want to go to Stonebury?' Tori asked.

Jasper shrugged. 'To be honest, I didn't get the chance to ask her. I think it's definitely worth keeping it as an option, though. I mean, it's hard to predict what the media reaction will be. These days, a child out of wedlock isn't nearly so much of a big deal. But keeping it a secret for so many years...'

'There's a story there, and they'll want to tell it.'

'Exactly.'

'How are you…how are you feeling?' Tori asked, after a moment, and Jasper couldn't shake the sensation that there was something more than concern behind the question. As if she was trying to get a read on a business competitor or something.

Either way, he didn't know how to answer.

'I… I don't know yet. It took me five years to come back here after I found out about Felix. And now learning that my mother knew all along, that she's not going to stop my father making it public… I haven't processed it all yet. I spoke to Felix earlier—for the first time in five years. I guess that maybe I'm coming to terms with the facts of it all, and that Felix, at least, wasn't to blame for what happened. But it's the lying and the secrets I can't move past. You know?'

'I know.' Tori's voice sounded raw, more than just an agreement. But before he could ask if *she* was okay, she pasted on a smile and held a hand out to him. 'Come on. We've got a party to get to. There'll be plenty of time for introspection and misery later.'

Her words were light, joking. But somehow they still sounded like a prediction.

And more than ever, Jasper felt the festive party spirit slipping away from him.

CHAPTER TWELVE

DOWNSTAIRS, THE PARTY was in full swing. The air hummed with classic Christmas tunes from the band, the singer a glamorous redhead who made everything sound sultry, and the waiters circulating with trays of champagne were being kept very busy. The Flaxstone Christmas party was always a highlight of the local social calendar—and normally of Tori's too. In a room full of people, she could forget that she was alone for Christmas, usually.

But not this year. This year, she felt more alone than she had since she'd left the Moorside, eight years ago. Because this year, she had someone to lose.

And she knew in her heart that she'd already lost him.

Jasper, returning son and heir, had been swept away by family, friends and acquaintances who hadn't seen him for five long years. He'd tried to keep her on his arm to start with, but she'd shaken her head and slipped away, indicating that she was heading for the canapés.

Mostly, she'd just needed to escape.

She needed to get everything straight in her head. A project list, the same way she always began any new project the earl delegated to her. Before she could start work, she needed to know the parameters.

Mentally, she ran through her usual checklist. After all, business was what she knew best—far more than people or relationships. And in the end, weren't they more or less the same thing? Interactions and negotiations and compromises—only on life choices and personal futures, rather than business proposals and property.

So, first up: what did she already know?

That was easy. She ticked them off in her head, half wishing she'd brought her notebook with her to write them down.

One. She knew that she felt more for Jasper than she'd felt for anyone since Tyler. A lot more. However much she'd tried to pretend to herself otherwise. She wouldn't be feeling this mixed up about the earl's offer otherwise.

Two. She knew that Jasper would be leaving for the States again in the new year. And she knew that she couldn't risk another long-distance relationship, not after Tyler.

Three. She knew that Jasper struggled to forgive even those he loved most. The man definitely knew how to hold a grudge.

Four. She knew that Jasper would feel betrayed if she left Flaxstone to run Stonebury with Felix. She couldn't fall in love with him, give him everything he needed, *and* go after what she needed too. She'd tried that before with Tyler, with disastrous results. This time, a relationship with Jasper—assuming that was even what he wanted—would mean either her leaving Flaxstone and the opportunity at Stonebury to be with him or…what? Asking him not to go back to a life he'd established overseas? To overlook the fact she was working with, supporting and hiding his half-brother—using the very plan she'd developed with him for protecting his mother? None of those options seemed likely.

So. Not a pretty picture so far. But there was one more thing she knew, too. She pulled a face as she made herself add it.

Five. She knew she wanted the job at Stonebury. She knew she was the best person for it, that it would rocket her career forward, and, most of all, she knew that she'd *earned* it.

Okay. They were the known factors. So, what *didn't* she know?

One. She didn't know how Jasper felt about

her. Oh, she knew that he *wanted* her, that much was obvious. But beyond that? She got the impression he was just as confused by it all as she was.

Was that it? If that was the only thing she didn't know—and, really, since Jasper was leaving anyway did it really matter how he felt?—then surely she should be able to make a decision on the information she had?

In fact, Tori knew deep down that she'd already made her choice. She'd felt it in the way she'd kept Jasper at arm's length—emotionally, if not physically—and she'd felt it sink in when he'd looked so confused by his mother's ability to forgive his father.

She wanted this job, this chance, and she couldn't give it up for someone who wasn't even staying around. And even if Jasper *could* forgive that, she wasn't going to even consider the idea of a long-distance relationship—not after what had happened the last time she'd tried it. In the end, the mistrust and the distance had destroyed not only her relationship with Tyler, but Tyler himself.

She needed to move on; she knew that now. The guilt was too heavy to hold onto for ever. But her heart ached too much to put it down. She didn't even know who she would be without it, after so long.

No. Better to end this thing with Jasper now, and move on with her solitary life. Box up the last couple of weeks and store them away in her heart with all the other painful memories, until she was strong enough to look at them again. One day.

With one last look to check that Jasper was still busy entertaining the guests, Tori slipped away to find the earl and tell him her decision.

And then she would go back to her cottage to pack.

She had a feeling that when Jasper found out, she'd be more welcome at the Moorside Inn than at Flaxstone, anyway.

The party was so busy, so loud, that it took Jasper some time to realise that Tori wasn't there any longer. He searched all the usual places—the buffet table, the dance floor, the quiet areas his mother set aside for conversation and flirtation—no sign of her. He even lingered outside the incredibly swanky portable bathrooms set up in the quad in case she was in there—although since she had access to a bedroom with its own bathroom upstairs it seemed unlikely. No Tori.

'Jasper!' His father's voice boomed out as he re-entered the ballroom where the main party was taking place. 'Let me introduce you to—'

'Have you seen Tori?' Jasper interrupted. 'I need to find her.' He *knew* there was something weird going on with her tonight. Why had he even let her out of his sight?

Because I'm not her boss. I have no control over where she goes or what she does. I'm not even her boyfriend; I don't even have the right to ask, *really.*

He should have talked to her earlier. Told her all the things he'd realised during his walk. Told her he was thinking of moving back home. That he didn't want to be without her any longer. More talking and less seduction might have meant that their positions were clearer and she might even have shared whatever was going on with her. But she'd displayed that long, slender back, naked under her dress, and he'd lost his mind over her. Again.

'Not since she told me the good news!' the earl said, raising his champagne glass in a happy mock toast.

Jasper froze. 'Good news?' All his instincts were screaming that whatever the news was, it wasn't going to be good for him. Otherwise she'd have told him first.

'Yes! That she's taking the job at Stonebury with Felix.' The earl's eyes widened a fraction. 'I assumed she'd spoken to you about it first...'

'Well, she hadn't,' Jasper snapped. Around

them, awkward partygoers were starting to sidle away, but he didn't care. Suddenly, things were falling into place. *This* was why she'd been distant upstairs, earlier. She'd already made her decision to leave, without even talking to him about it. He'd thought their lovemaking had been the start of something. But apparently Tori had been saying goodbye.

'When she said she needed time to consider, I interpreted that as a conversation between the two of you. I mean, it was obvious that you two were, well, fond of each other, and with you staying here at Flaxstone now—'

'I never said I was staying.' But he wanted to. He wanted to stay here with Tori. Or at Stonebury with her. Except she'd be there with Felix, apparently. The half-brother he hadn't even managed a full and unstilted conversation with, yet. The one she'd chosen over him all the same.

This wasn't a steak and ale pie she was stealing. She'd taken their whole plan, the project they'd designed for his mother, and handed it over to Felix instead, without even considering him.

'Well, maybe that's why Tori didn't talk to you about it, then,' the earl said, far too reasonably for Jasper's liking. 'If you're not here what does it matter where she goes?'

'You *know* why it matters.' Anger was rising through him now, red hot as it burned through his chest, up his throat and out of his mouth. 'We planned Stonebury as an escape for Mother, you know that. And now you're taking whatever you want and screwing it all up again, just like you did nearly thirty years ago. You always want everything, don't you? To have your cake and eat it. You wanted to marry Mother for her money, and you wanted your mistress on the side. You wanted your legal heir and your illegitimate son growing up together, even if neither of them knew the truth. And now you want to tell the world that Felix is your son and damn the consequences for anyone else, and even if it means stealing away the woman I'm falling in love with from me.'

It was the gasps—those sharp intakes of breath that spoke of total shock—that made Jasper realise he was shouting. And the instant chatter that followed that alerted him to what he'd actually said.

Oh, God. He was in love with Tori Edwards. When the hell had *that* happened?

The minute she kissed you, you idiot, his brain retorted.

But it wasn't until he turned and saw Felix and Tori standing in the open doorway, their eyes wide with horror, that he realised what it all meant.

'Well, son,' his father said softly. 'I think you've outdone me this time, don't you?'

Jasper blinked, and Tori and Felix were gone, probably running away, but he couldn't even blame them. Who told a woman they loved her in front of an entire party while yelling at their father and spilling family secrets? Although, in fairness, he hadn't known he was going to say it until it was out there.

He hadn't even known he felt it. But now, looking back at their meandering relationship...it seemed impossible that he'd ever *not* known. When he'd returned to Flaxstone, he'd thought Tori was just unfinished business— one night that could have been more but never got the chance to be.

But now he knew better. He knew she was his future. Or she could have been.

'Yes, Dad,' he said, his voice faint. 'This time it's all me.'

And he wasn't even sure he deserved forgiveness.

Tori hoisted her overnight bag onto her shoulder as she stormed down the path to her cottage, Felix hurrying after her.

'Are you this furious with him on my behalf

or on your own?' Felix asked as she fumbled with the key in her lock. 'Because, you know, this wasn't exactly how I wanted the news to come out, for sure. But he said he loved you.'

'Because he's trying to make me feel guilty about taking the job. Or manipulate me into turning it down, one or the other. I've been here before.'

She knew how this went. She'd been exactly here with Tyler, and she wasn't going to let herself get caught up in it again.

'Or because…he really means it?' Felix suggested, eyebrows raised.

Tori sighed. She liked Felix, really she did. But considering his birth and upbringing he had a surprisingly uncomplicated view of the world. Opening her front door, she tried to find the familiar sensation of home. Of security.

It wasn't there.

She stepped inside anyway, turning back to stop Felix on the threshold.

'Look, I appreciate you trying to help, but unless you want to do my packing for me you might as well go back to the party.' She caught the uncomfortable look on his face and realised: he couldn't go back either. Everyone would be talking about him and him being there wouldn't stop that. If anything, it would make it worse.

Yeah, maybe Felix *was* having a worse night than her.

Fumbling with her key ring, she removed a silver key and pressed it into his palm. 'Sneak in through the locked garage entrance, and head up to the Yellow Room,' she suggested. 'I'm not going to be using it again tonight.'

'Are you sure?'

'Very.' She wasn't going back to Flaxstone Hall tonight. Or possibly at all, until she was sure that Jasper was safely on another continent. 'Wait!' She took another key from the ring and handed it to him.

'Why do I need your cottage key?'

'Just…in case,' she said. She didn't know in case of what—or didn't want to think about it. *In case I never come back.* 'And maybe you could water my Christmas tree while I'm gone?'

Felix rolled his eyes, but took the key and left. As she shed her dress and changed into normal clothes, grabbing her overnight bag, Tori felt a pang of guilt for leaving Felix to weather this night on his own, but she had to get moving fast, before Jasper—

A hammering on the door interrupted the thought.

Too late.

Taking a deep, steadying breath, Tori opened

the door, grateful at least that she'd changed out of her evening dress and into a more professional, and comfortable, pair of black trousers and sweater. She had made a work decision. And that was what this conversation needed to be about.

'Tori. I… Can I come in?'

With a short nod, she stepped aside to let him enter. 'But I don't have long,' she said, turning her back on him as she returned to her packing. 'I want to get to the Moorside before last orders.'

For so many years, the thought of the inn had driven her away. But suddenly, it was the only place she wanted to be.

'You're going? Really? I thought— Is this because of the job, or because of what I said?'

'Both, to be honest.' She just needed to get away. Why couldn't he understand that?

She'd rather take the pain in Uncle Henry's eyes than the anger she expected to see in Jasper's.

'Look, I know I shouldn't have blurted out what I said that way. It's no excuse, but my father told me about the job offer at Stonebury— you running the place with Felix—and I guess I was hurt that you didn't talk to me about it first—'

'Why would I?' she interrupted.

She couldn't let him say too much, or she risked him saying all the things that could sway her, change her mind, as Tyler had tried to do.

I love you. I can't do it without you. It'll all be your fault if you go and leave me.

'It was a work decision, but not one I had an obligation to discuss with you as a colleague. Especially as a colleague who will also be leaving soon.'

Jasper looked as if she'd slapped him in the face. 'What if I wasn't? Leaving, I mean?'

He was planning on staying? Tori shook her head. It didn't change anything. It *couldn't* change anything. The physical distance between them was only one problem. The emotional gulf was far bigger.

She hadn't moved on from Tyler's death, and *neither* of them knew how to forgive— others or themselves. How could they start a relationship there?

She had to end this, now, before her heart broke too much. 'Then you'll stay and be furious at your family and at me for all time, and I'm sure that will be just brilliant for all of us, but I'll be at Stonebury helping the brother you just exposed to the world keep out of the limelight for a while.'

That stopped him. '*That's* why you took the job? Because you wanted to help Felix?'

'I took the job because I wanted the job. Because I deserved the job.'

'And you didn't care how I felt about it.' Jasper's expression hardened.

Of course she cared. But she couldn't let him see how much. 'Jasper, we've slept together twice. Three times if you count five years ago. It's hardly a lasting relationship. You can't expect me to make decisions about my career and my future based on it.' Not the way Tyler had. Expecting her to give up all her hopes for her future, her ambition, for a teenage relationship she couldn't even be sure would last. Now Jasper was asking her to do the same, but it was different this time.

She hadn't made Jasper any promises. Hadn't told him she loved him. And Jasper... he was stronger than Tyler had been. He'd be fine without her.

It was her own heart she was worried about.

'Maybe not,' he admitted. 'But as a friend I would expect you to talk to me before running away.'

'Like you did to Felix five years ago?' she shot back.

Jasper swore under his breath, raking his hands through his hair as he visibly tried to calm himself. That was no good. She didn't want him calm. She wanted him gone, so she could run far away and let her heart break in peace.

He wasn't offering her for ever. He was offering her exactly what Tyler had—a possibility of love as long as she did what he wanted. And she wasn't going to take that risk.

Still, when Jasper spoke again, his voice was softer, calmer. 'Look, Tori, I should have told you I was planning on staying at Flaxstone. I meant to, tonight. And I'm going to work on my relationship with my family, really I am.'

'But will you ever forgive them? Would you ever forgive me, if I went to Stonebury with Felix?' Because that was what it all came down to. Forgiveness. She couldn't forgive Tyler for what he'd done, and she couldn't forgive herself for letting him. And Jasper couldn't forgive the lies and betrayal that had driven him away from his home in the first place.

How could they start any kind of a relationship when they were both so filled with resentment? Maybe they weren't good people like Lady Flaxstone. Maybe they weren't meant to forgive.

But that just meant that one day they'd do something to each other that couldn't be forgiven either. Far better to cut this off now and avoid that pain later.

'I'm… I'm trying, Tori. I… I said I love you. Isn't that enough? Enough for you to stay and work this out with me?'

'You love me?' She shook her head. 'Jasper, you don't even know me. If you did, you'd know that love isn't ever enough. Love just forces us down roads we don't want to walk, and makes us feel guilty for wanting the things we want. I've been here before, and I know how this ends. I've had enough of love, thanks.'

With that, she turned away and walked into her bedroom to finish packing. And tried to pretend that her heart wasn't breaking. Because for once, just once, she wished that love really *could* be enough.

CHAPTER THIRTEEN

'YOU REALISE THIS isn't at all healthy, right?' Felix's voice cut through the quiet of the snowy countryside three days later, and Jasper looked up suddenly from his seat on the bench outside Tori's cottage.

'I'm enjoying the miracle of a white Christmas in Britain. Besides, it's quiet here,' he said defensively. 'There's a seat, no one bothers me, and it's not like Tori's here to object.' He had a lot of thinking to do, and he found he thought best somewhere he couldn't hear his father's voice.

Although at least the earl's jolly tones drowned out the sound of Tori tearing down everything he'd hoped for, playing on a loop inside his head. But Jasper couldn't shake the feeling that he deserved to hear it. That if he replayed that moment enough, he'd find the key to fixing it. Something she'd said, something he'd missed.

So far, however, he was mostly just depressing himself.

'Tori not being here is exactly why it's getting kind of creepy, you sitting outside her empty cottage every day.'

'Not every day,' Jasper lied. Felix raised his eyebrows at him, and he sighed. 'Fine. Every day. I just... I can't think straight up at the hall.'

'I know the feeling.'

Jasper winced as Felix brushed the snow off the bench and sat down beside him. Jasper just had to contend with his father's pointed comments about his loyal deputy's absence. Felix had to cope with the media on the phone, the Internet covering every aspect of his life so far, and all sorts of acquaintances he barely knew popping out of the woodwork to get in his good graces, now he was set to inherit a significant portion of the Flaxstone estate and bank accounts.

'Did I mention I'm sorry for outing you at the party?'

'Yes,' Felix said. 'Many times. But do feel free to mention it again. You can throw in a bonus apology for running away five years ago too, if you like.'

'Sorry,' Jasper said again. He seemed to be saying it a lot. But he also seemed to be rebuilding bridges he'd thought were damaged beyond repair. Maybe he and Felix wouldn't ever be best friends the way they had been once, but perhaps instead they'd be something more.

Brothers, even.

It was weird, in a way, to go from the man who couldn't forgive the lies he'd been told, to the one who needed to ask for forgiveness. But maybe that was the lesson he'd been meant to learn all along: that forgiving and asking forgiveness were two sides of the same coin, and everyone needed to do both from time to time.

He wished he could ask Tori for forgiveness, even if he wasn't entirely sure what he'd done wrong. Wished he could forgive her for leaving, but he wasn't there yet, however much he was learning.

He didn't *understand*. How could he forgive what didn't make any sense?

He hadn't understood how his parents could lie to him for so long, or how Felix could keep the truth from him after he'd found out, but he was starting to, now. When love and family and everything was so fragile, people did what they had to in order to keep it together. He wouldn't have understood that at seventeen, when Felix learned the truth.

But he didn't think he would ever understand how Tori could walk away from the connection between them, when he was offering to change his whole life, his whole existence for her. How she could hear him say he loved her, and have it mean nothing.

Maybe he should have told her about the last time he'd said that to a woman, only to have her turn round and humiliate him. Maybe then she'd realise how much it meant to him.

Or maybe not. His first love had ended in embarrassment. Hers had ended in death. She wasn't likely to cut him much slack for that.

And anyway, *she* was the one who had left. Maybe she should be running back and begging *him* for forgiveness.

'You *could* go after her, you realise,' Felix said after a moment. 'It's not like you don't know where she is.'

'It's also not as if she gave me any indication at all that she wanted me to follow her,' Jasper pointed out. 'I told her I loved her—'

'No, you told a party full of strangers you loved her, mostly to make our father feel guilty.'

Our father. That still sounded strange.

'It doesn't matter. She said love isn't enough.' But it was all he had to give.

The realisation had been a slow one, creeping in between snow falls and frozen rivers, silent in the muffled winter landscape. Eight years ago when they'd met, she'd been a challenge. Five years ago, when they'd first spent the night together, she'd been a refuge. Two weeks ago, when they'd been stranded together at the Moorside, she'd still been a mystery—but one he was piecing together the clues to make sense of. By the time she'd kissed him at the Christmas market, she'd been all he could think about. She'd become a friend, then something more, something deeper, something he was scared to name unless it escaped again.

He'd barely known he was falling until he was all in. Like slipping on ice.

Yes, that was a perfect description for how falling in love with Tori Edwards felt. As if his feet had gone from under him and he was flat on his back on the hard, icy ground wondering what the hell just happened.

'She said something else, before you got to the cottage. Something that made about as much sense as all of that did.' Felix's brows knitted together as he obviously tried to remember it word for word. 'She said she'd been here before. That you were just saying you loved her to try and get her to stay, or make her feel guilty or something.'

'She thought I was only proclaiming love in the most embarrassing way possible to make her feel bad?' Jasper's brain caught up with the rest of what Felix had said. 'Wait. She said she'd been here before?'

'That's what she said.'

Yes. She'd said that to him, too, but he hadn't realised the significance of it until now. He'd assumed she was talking about the first time they'd slept together, just before he'd left the country. But what if she wasn't?

Because she *hadn't* been here with him before. This was all different, this time. He'd definitely never told her he loved her before. And, given what else he knew about her love life and relationship history, that left him only one possible candidate.

'Tyler.'

'Who?' Felix asked.

'Her ex-boyfriend. The son of her sort-of foster parents. He died, before she came here. But I'm starting to think there was more to that story than she told me.' He'd known that—or sensed it at least—before. But he hadn't imagined it could be something big enough to derail everything between them.

'Isn't there always?'

'Maybe I just wasn't asking the right questions.' And maybe he needed to.

No more secrets. That was what he'd promised himself when he came back here. He just hadn't anticipated the challenge that was Tori Edwards and her defensive walls.

Jasper sprang to his feet, and Felix followed. 'You're going to go see her?'

'I'm going to go see her.'

'Hang on, then.' Felix fished a key from his pocket and let himself into Tori's cottage.

'Wait, why do you have a key to her cottage?' Jasper called from the doorstep, reluctant to go inside without Tori's permission even though she wasn't there.

'She wanted me to water her Christmas tree,' Felix yelled back.

'Of course she did.'

Felix re-emerged moments later with a parcel wrapped in Christmas paper; one Jasper recognised. It was the one Henry had given him for Tori when they'd left the Moorside, just a couple of weeks ago now.

'It's Christmas Day. She'll want this,' Felix said.

Jasper nodded, and took the parcel from him. 'I'll deliver it. Make my excuses with the parents for Christmas dinner?'

'Of course. Just be careful on the roads,' Felix said. 'There's more snow forecast. And I don't want to lose a brother when I only just got him back.'

'Neither do I.' Jasper flashed him a grin,

then ran for his four-by-four, parked up in the garage by the house.

It was time to put an end to all the secrets. It was time to bring Tori home again.

Tori stared at the door in front of her, willing herself to open it.

She'd been back at the Moorside for three days now. It was time.

She just still didn't quite feel ready.

Aunt Liz and Uncle Henry had looked about as surprised as she'd expected when she'd appeared on their doorstep three nights ago. For all they'd asked her to come back for Christmas, it was clear they hadn't actually expected that she *would*. Still, Liz had made up her room for her, and Henry had fed her dinner—'Anything but pie?' she'd asked, at which question he'd given her a knowing look—and she'd settled back into life at the Moorside as if she'd never left.

Well, almost.

'Are you going to go in?' Henry's voice behind her made her jump. 'Only, our turkey will be ready in six hours, and I'd hate for you to miss it because you're busy staring at a door.'

Not just any door. Tyler's door.

Henry sank down against the wall to sit beside her on the floor, their legs stretched out across the hallway ahead of them. The pub was still open, for all that it was Christmas Day, but all the lunches were cooked and being served. Another couple of hours and all that would be left was mopping up the last of the drinkers before sending them home to their families and having their own, very late, Christmas dinner.

'He loved you so much, you know,' Henry said. 'He'd want you to move on and be happy, if that's what this is about.'

'It's not.' Tori considered. 'Well, not entirely.'

Yes, she felt guilty about moving on and leaving Tyler behind, but then, she'd been feeling that guilt since long before he'd died. Weirdly, she didn't feel as if she was betraying Tyler with Jasper. If anything, she felt she was betraying Jasper, by clinging onto Tyler's memory.

She'd done a lot of thinking over the last three days, and one thing was crystal clear to her. If she wanted to move on—with Jasper, or with anyone—she needed to put Tyler's ghost to rest.

And the only way she'd been able to come up with to do that was by telling the truth.

'Did he ever talk to you, about me leaving for university?' Tori asked. She'd never spoken with Tyler's parents about what had happened before she'd left, or after. But suddenly, she wondered if they knew anyway. They'd loved their son deeply, but they'd never claimed he was perfect. None of them were.

All of them needed forgiveness, she realised now. But the dead couldn't give it.

'He didn't want you to go, I know that,' Henry admitted. 'But I told him then, if you truly love her, son, you have to let her go. She has great things in her and she has to go and achieve them. She'll come back when she's ready, but not if we hold on too tight.'

Tori looked away from the door and stared at the man who had chosen to be her uncle, even when blood didn't make him one. 'You told him that?'

'Yep. Bet he didn't listen though.' He shook his head. 'I loved that boy more than my own life, and it kills me every day that he's gone. But he never listened to a word of advice his whole life.'

'He…he begged me not to go. Told me if I truly loved him, I'd stay. That leaving would break him. He said…he said he was scared he'd do something stupid if I wasn't there.' Henry's expression hardened at her words, but she pressed on. She needed to say this. Needed to get it all out, at last. No more secrets. 'I told him I had to go—that if I gave up this opportunity I'd never forgive myself. I thought we could carry on together anyway; you remember, I came back every weekend that first term to see him.'

'I remember.' Henry's voice was dark. He already knew how the story ended, of course. 'Liz was worried. She thought you should be spending more time making new friends at university.'

'Every time I came back it got harder. Tyler…he seemed more and more unstable. Accusing me of cheating on him. Of laughing at him, when I was away. He kept telling me that if I went back to university without him he didn't know what he'd do. That he wouldn't be responsible for what happened.' The implication had been clear. Whatever stupid thing Tyler did without her there to stop him would be her fault. Her responsibility.

'And then he went out, got drunk, and tried to drive home.' Henry rubbed a hand across his wrinkled brow, looking older and more tired than Tori had ever imagined he could look. Then he stretched out his arm and wrapped it around her shoulder, pulling her close against him as they both stared at Tyler's bedroom door, and remembered the boy they had lost.

'He was an idiot,' Henry said after a moment. 'And that wasn't your fault, not for a moment. I… I'm angry with him now, and I'd have been furious with him then if I'd known what was going on. But at least I know now. And I can tell you what happened to Tyler wasn't your fault. Not in any way, shape or form.'

'But if I hadn't gone—'

'Then maybe it would have happened later, or differently, or not at all. But it still wouldn't have been your fault. He made his choices and some of them were terrible ones, and he paid the price for that. He should never have tried to make you carry that blame.'

'We both made choices,' Tori pointed out. 'I chose to leave him behind, even though I knew it could be the end of our relationship.' It hurt to admit that; that she'd chosen her own ambition and future over the boy who was supposed to be the love of her life.

'You were only eighteen,' Henry replied. 'And you made the right choice. You couldn't mortgage your whole future for a teenage relationship that probably wouldn't last anyway. And if it was meant to be, it would have been. If it was meant to be he would have supported you every step of the way. I'm ashamed that he didn't.'

Tori lowered her head as she shook it, too

overcome to find words, her eyes burning with unshed tears.

'This is why you didn't come back here after the funeral, isn't it?' Henry said. 'Why you stayed away so long. I always wondered… Liz said it probably just hurt too much to be here with all the memories, but I suspected it must have been something more.'

'I thought you'd blame me, if you knew the truth. *I* blamed me.' She took a shuddering breath. 'I thought you'd hate me, and it hurt so much I couldn't face it.'

In all honesty, it *still* hurt. Maybe her first visit back to the Moorside in the snow and the dark had started to soothe some of the pain, but the guilt still hung on.

'You're our family, every bit as much as Tyler was, even if it is by love, not blood.' Henry hugged her tighter. 'We could never do anything but love you, the same way we'll always love Tyler, even if we don't agree with his choices. But in *your* case, you made the right choice going. Staying away…that choice I'm less keen on.'

'So you *are* mad at me?'

'No. I *missed* you.' Henry sighed. 'Maybe I'm not saying this right. What I mean is… Vicky, Liz and I will always forgive you and always love you, even if we don't agree with you. You're family and you will always have a home here.'

That was all it took to send her over the edge. The tears cascaded over her cheeks as she buried her head against Henry's chest, her body shaking with sobs as he held her. As if the guilt and the self-loathing were leaving her in the flood of tears. Washing her soul clean.

She was truly home again, at last.

It took a while for her to regain her composure. But when she did, she wiped her eyes, kissed Henry on the cheek, and straightened her back as she stood again, ready to enter Tyler's room at last.

It was time to say goodbye, for the last time.

And then she had a new life to say hello to, she hoped.

CHAPTER FOURTEEN

FELIX HADN'T BEEN kidding about the snow.

Thick, heavy flakes landed on his windscreen faster than his wipers could clear them, and Jasper peered through the glass at a world turning whiter by the moment. The air swirled and rushed with snow, whipped up by a wild wind that whistled down the valleys and around the rocks of the moors.

Somewhere up ahead was the Moorside Inn and the woman he loved.

Now he just had to get to her. And not crash on the way.

A shiver went through him at the thought. From what she'd said, he knew he couldn't be far from where Tyler had died. The last thing Tori needed was another man to mourn.

He slowed the car to a crawl. Maybe it would take him longer, but he'd get there in one piece, at least.

He was just picking out the landmarks that

he knew led to the Moorside Inn when he saw the blue flashing lights. Easing onto the brakes, he slowed a good distance away from them, glad that the date—Christmas Day— meant the roads were mostly clear. Unfastening his seat belt, he pulled the hood of his coat over his head and ducked out of the car to find out what was happening.

'Tree down in the road, sir.' Was that the same young policeman who'd visited the Moorside last time? Jasper had a feeling it might be. The last few weeks seemed to be coming full circle. Squinting through the snow, he could see the heavy, old tree trunk spanning the whole width of the road. A set of headlights on the other side showed that his wasn't the only Christmas Day not going to plan.

'Going to be closed until they clear it,' the police officer continued. 'You might want to turn round and go back the way you came, if you can make it through the snow.'

Jasper looked back down the road he'd just travelled, and saw the weather closing in behind him. But more than that, he saw all the distance and pain and anger that had filled his last five years. The lack of forgiveness, the burning sense of injustice eating away at him.

He didn't want to go that way.

'I'll park up and keep going on foot,' he said. 'I know an inn you can shelter at for the night. If you like.'

He knew that voice. He loved that voice.

Jasper spun to find Tori leaning against the fallen tree, a bright red hat pulled down low over her dark hair, and a hopeful smile on her face.

He'd never seen anything so beautiful.

'That would be wonderful,' he said, stepping closer. 'Any chance it serves steak and ale pie?' He could almost take her in his arms, but he still wasn't completely sure that was what she wanted. Although the fact that she was here, in the snow, on this road…had she been trying to reach him, too? He hoped so. But either way, the next move had to be hers.

'It might. But it's Christmas Day so, mostly turkey and trimmings, I think.' She took a step too, and suddenly she was so close he could see the snowflakes landing on her eyelashes. She blinked them away, and met his gaze, and he knew.

He knew that he had to convince this woman to give him a chance. Maybe she'd never be able to love him, and he'd have to let her go. But if there was any chance she might want to stay in his life for always…he had to try.

'Tori, I… I'm sorry. For everything. I've

learned a lot about forgiveness recently—most of it from you, in a roundabout way. You were right, about so many things. I've talked a lot with Felix, and with my parents, especially since you left. And while I'm still not all the way there, I'm trying, really, I am. And I hope that you—'

He broke off as she placed an icy hand against his cheek. Then she stretched up on tiptoe and pressed her cold lips to his. 'Yes,' she murmured, barely pulling away at all. 'Yes to all of it. Now come on. Let's get out of the cold.'

Henry and Liz barely even looked surprised at all this time when she turned up with Jasper in tow, his car parked out of the way on the side of the road to worry about later. They had more important things to deal with now.

'Here for the turkey, I suppose?' Henry asked Jasper, holding out a hand for him to shake.

'Not just the turkey,' Jasper replied, smiling down at her. Tori tried not to blush, but from Liz's soppy smile she was pretty sure she'd failed.

She'd talked to her aunt, too, after she'd made her peace with Tyler, talking to him as if he'd never left his childhood bedroom. Maybe he hadn't, in essence. But when she'd closed the door behind her for the last time, she knew she, at least, had pulled whatever part of her heart that had stayed in the past with him fully into the future. Liz had hugged her tight and told her that she should listen to her uncle. Tori was family, and that was the end of the matter.

And now, as she sat around the best table in the inn, all the other patrons gone, with Jasper at her side and Liz and Henry across from her, Tori started to truly believe that maybe she *could* be part of a family again. That she could forgive herself and start over.

And it started here, now, this Christmas Day, somewhere she'd never expected to be again with someone she'd never imagined she could like, let alone love.

But she did—love Jasper. She hadn't told him yet, and she hugged the truth of it deep inside her. She had a feeling this would be one secret he wouldn't object to. Maybe it could even be her Christmas present to him.

She couldn't pinpoint the moment she'd fallen in love with him, but maybe she didn't have to. He'd crept under her defences, finding holes she hadn't known existed while she'd been trying desperately to build the walls higher so he couldn't climb them. However he'd got inside her heart, he'd helped to crowd out the old feelings that had filled it, and brought in fresh, new ones.

Like hope.

They still had a long way to go, and many, many walls to climb. But this time, she had hope that they could do it together.

She wanted to get Jasper alone. She wanted to tell him everything, to listen to everything he had to say. But it was Christmas Day—her first Christmas Day with her family in eight long years—and there were traditions to be followed at the Moorside Inn. Ones even love couldn't delay.

Christmas dinner was everything she remembered from her childhood: crackers and terrible jokes and stupid hats and the most delicious dinner anyone ever ate because Henry saved all the best bits for them. The tree lights twinkled in the corner, and festive tunes played softly from the speaker system. It was nothing at all like the fancy Christmas party at Flaxstone Hall, but it felt more magical to Tori.

'Your parents don't mind you joining us for Christmas dinner?' Liz asked as they all tucked in.

Jasper shook his head as he chewed a mouthful of turkey. 'I asked my…my brother to explain to them why I had to go. I think they'll understand.' He shot Tori a look that made her mouth dry, and had her reaching for her wine glass. In fact, she was so distracted it took her a whole swallow to realise that he'd called Felix his brother.

Seemed he really had made progress while she was gone.

But finally, *finally*, dinner was over. Liz and Henry shooed off their offers of help to clear up, and suddenly they were upstairs in her old bedroom, staring at each other across that damn single bed again.

At least we won't mind cosying up nearly so much this time...

'I'm sorry I ran away from Flaxstone,' Tori started, when Jasper seemed content to just look at her, his eyes warm and wanting. 'Away from you. I just... I told you about Tyler. How he died when I went away to university. But I never told you everything and... I think it's time that I did.'

Jasper blinked, then reached out a hand to take hers and sat them down beside each other on the bed. 'Tell me everything.'

And she did. Everything she'd told Henry, everything she'd been keeping trapped inside her for eight long years.

'In the end, I just knew it was my fault that he'd died,' she said, once she'd explained the whole story. 'I'd chosen my ambition and my future over my relationship with him, and he'd done something stupid, just like he'd warned me he would. That's why I couldn't come back here, couldn't move on, couldn't find love again. Because I knew my choices had killed him and—worse still—I knew I'd make the same choices again if I had to.'

Jasper shook his head. 'No. *His* choices led him to that car accident. He chose to drive after drinking—you didn't make him do that. And if he really loved you, he wouldn't have tried to scare and threaten you out of going after your dreams. He'd have lifted you up to help you chase them.'

'I'm starting to see that now,' Tori admitted. 'But when I thought you were leaving the country again, I knew I couldn't risk my heart on a long-distance relationship, which meant I couldn't risk falling for you at all. And then when your father offered me the job at Stonebury... I knew I was about to do the same thing that I'd done to Tyler all over again. Take the opportunity I wanted so badly, even though I knew it would hurt you. And I was so damned scared that it seemed better to run away before you could talk me out of it. Before anyone got hurt.'

'It wasn't the same,' Jasper said. 'But...but I

wish you'd felt you could talk to me about it. That we could discuss it and come up with an answer together.'

'I just couldn't. I still had Tyler's ghost in my head. Until I laid that to rest, anything between us was impossible.'

'But you have done that now?' Jasper asked.

'I...hope so. I suspect these things are a work in progress.' She had to be honest, now most of all. Even if the answer wasn't the one she really wanted to give.

'Like rebuilding a family riddled with secrets, lies and abandonment.' Jasper gave her a half-smile. 'And I get it. I understand why you couldn't talk to me—even without Tyler's ghost whispering lies at you. I hadn't exactly shown myself to be the most understanding and forgiving of boyfriends, anyway.'

'Boyfriends?'

He shrugged. 'Well, if you'll have me.'

Tori tilted her head and considered him. He was gorgeous, rich, he made her whole body hum with wanting him, and he made paper chains with bored kids.

'I suppose I could do worse. I have conditions, though.'

'Why am I not surprised?' Leaning back against the bedhead, he pulled her up into his arms, and she twisted so she could still see his face. It was less comfortable than just nuzzling up to him, but Tori knew they had to look each other in the eye as they made these decisions together.

No more secrets between them, now. And not ever.

'Go on, then,' he said.

'No running away when things get tough—and, yes, I know that one goes for me too,' she said, before he could even open his mouth the whole way. 'We talk about things instead of, well, our usual way of doing things.'

'Holding grudges and feeling guilty? Yeah, I guess talking *does* sound a more sensible plan.' He gave her a gentle smile and kissed the top of her head. Tori leaned into his shoulder, feeling stronger just from the touch of him.

'And we forgive when we mess things up,' Jasper added. 'That's my condition. Because we're not going to get things right all the time, either of us. *Especially* us. But you're right. We don't run. And we forgive—each other and ourselves.'

For him, she knew the first would be a challenge. For her, it would probably be the second. But she figured that together they might even balance each other out.

'Okay,' she agreed. 'Number one rule: forgive, always.' She placed a kiss just where his shirt collar sat open, and let herself rest her head for a moment.

'And please…' He placed a finger under her chin and tilted it so she was looking at him again. 'Don't pull up that drawbridge again? I spent so long trying to get behind those battlements…when you put all your defences back up on me that night at the party, I honestly thought that was it. That I was back out in the cold for good.'

'I'm sorry. I just—'

'I understand why you did it,' he interrupted her. 'I'm not asking for apologies. I just need you to know…you don't have to do that any more. Not with me. There's nothing you need to hide from me, and no need for the armour. I'm all in, Tori. I didn't expect to be—I came home thinking I'd be leaving again, and quick. But instead I got snowed in with you and my whole world changed. Because I saw behind your armour and I realised that was all I wanted to do. Solve the puzzle of Tori Edwards. And now I know I could happily spend the rest of my life doing just that, if you'll let me.'

His eyes were so serious, so sincere, that Tori's heart rose until she had to swallow it back down. 'Let's start with figuring out the puzzle of fitting both of us in this bed, shall we?' She smiled gently, letting him know she wasn't turning down everything he was offering. 'Take it one day—or night—at a time.'

He returned her smile. 'Yeah. One day at a time.' Then his grin turned wicked. 'And I definitely have some ideas about the bed-sharing thing…'

He wrapped an arm around her waist and tipped her flat on her back, smothering her squeal with a kiss. And Tori knew that if they could just keep talking, and forgiving, everything was going to be just fine.

Better than fine. Life was going to be wonderful again.

EPILOGUE

STONEBURY HALL LOOKED at its best in the snow, Jasper decided.

All spring and summer they'd worked on getting the estate into shape; setting up the barns for the craft stalls and workshops, getting the tea room ready for its first customers—not to mention doing up the house itself.

But now that Christmas was almost here again, a full year since he and Tori had first walked the grounds of this strange, crenellated hall in the snow, it felt as if *this* was how the place was always meant to be.

'Did you imagine for a moment, a year ago, that we'd be here now?' he asked as he and Tori stood, gloved hand in gloved hand, looking up at the battlements and stone walls of their new home.

Tori gave him her usual 'are you crazy?' look. He was actually surprisingly fond of it these days.

'Me? Absolutely. I figured I'd be here making a huge success of the business. You? Not so much.'

Rolling his eyes, Jasper nudged her in the ribs, wondering if she even felt it through all the layers of coat and clothes between them. She squirmed out of the way and laughed, all the same.

'Okay, fine, I hadn't exactly anticipated us living here together, spending *Christmas* here. But then, I didn't imagine spending last Christmas at the Moorside, either.'

'Last Christmas was perfect.' Maybe it hadn't started out that way, but by the end it had been everything he'd ever wanted—even if he hadn't known until that very moment that he wanted it. Tori had given him a chance to spend the rest of his life learning her, loving her. And they hadn't gone into it with more secrets, more hidden expectations. They'd gone in openly, knowing what they needed from each other—and from themselves.

Which wasn't to say it had all been plain sailing. They'd still had to navigate the revelations of Felix's parentage—which society and the gossip magazines had enjoyed as much as Jasper had feared. But Felix had gone with Tori to Stonebury as their father had planned, and managed to stay out of the limelight, until things had at least started to blow over.

Jasper, meanwhile, had been required to go back to the States and tidy up his affairs there before he could move back to Britain full time. Neither he nor Tori had been happy about the idea of a long-distance relationship, especially given Tori's previous experiences, but they'd made it work.

Well, actually they'd been miserable, and bickered for a lot of it. But they'd visited when they could, forgiven each other when things got too much, and they'd made it through.

And now they were here, about to spend their first Christmas at Stonebury. The Christmas village had been doing a roaring trade for months, and even in the summer some of the festive workshops had proved popular. There was still a lot of work to do to make the place a long-standing success, but Jasper had faith that Tori could do it. This project was her baby, after all.

And he…well, he'd be getting back to working with his father in the new year, and with Felix. The earl had announced, rather impatiently upon Jasper's return, that he *did* want to retire one day, and his sons needed to be ready to take over his empire.

So they were all working together. Which

would be *interesting*. But with Tori to come home to every night, and a promise that there were no more secrets to worry about, Jasper had faith that it could work. Hopefully.

'I'm just glad that Henry's coming to cook us Christmas dinner,' Tori said, shivering a little beside him. Her aunt and uncle had taken the unprecedented step of actually closing the Moorside Inn in order to join them for Christmas. Jasper hoped that was a sign of how far Tori's relationship with them had come in the last twelve months.

'Do you think steak and ale pie could be considered a traditional Christmas dish?' he asked hopefully.

Laughing, Tori shook her head. 'Not even a little bit. But when they get here, you might want to put your Christmas present in the fridge straight away. Henry has a soft spot for you, I think.'

Jasper beamed. 'Christmas with the woman I love, and my family, in my new home, and with steak and ale pie. I can only think of one more thing that would make this the absolutely perfect Christmas.'

'More than steak and ale pie?' Tori asked, eyebrows raised.

'Yep.' Jasper reached into his coat pocket and pulled out the ring box his mother had given him, last time he'd seen her at Flaxstone. He handed it to Tori, who opened it with a gasp. 'Marry me? I can't promise it will always be easy, but I *can* promise I'll make it worth it. Because I love you, and I want to spend my whole life showing you that.'

Tori looked up at him, tears at the corners of her eyes. 'Of course I'll marry you.'

'Really?'

'Absolutely. Because I love you too, and the last year has shown me that love isn't what I thought it was. That *I'm* not who I thought I was.' She gave him a wicked grin. 'Besides, if we're married, half your steak and ale pies become mine, so—'

She shrieked as he wrapped his arms around her middle, lifting her to kiss her thoroughly. And then he did it again for good measure.

Because he'd solved the first part of the puzzle of Tori Edwards; who she was now and what she needed.

And he knew he'd spend the rest of his live figuring out how to keep her as happy as he was right now.

Even if it meant sharing his steak and ale pies.

* * * * *

If you enjoyed this story,
check out these other great reads
from Sophie Pembroke

Pregnant on the Earl's Doorstep
Carrying Her Millionaire's Baby
CEO's Marriage Miracle
Road Trip with the Best Man

All available now!